P9-CNB-207

ALSO BY ELIE WIESEL

Night

Dawn

The Accident

The Town Beyond the Wall

The Gates of the Forest

The Jews of Silence

Legends of Our Time

A Beggar in Jerusalem

One Generation After

Souls on Fire

The Oath

Ani Maamin (cantata)

Zalmen, or The Madness of God (play)

Messengers of God

A Jew Today

Four Hasidic Masters

The Trial of God (play)

The Testament

Five Biblical Portraits

Somewhere a Master

The Golem (illustrated by Mark Podwal)

The Fifth Son

Against Silence (edited by Irving Abrahamson)

Twilight

The Six Days of Destruction (with Albert Friedlander)

A Journey into Faith (conversations with John Cardinal O'Connor)

From the Kingdom of Memory

Sages and Dreamers

The Forgotten

A Passover Haggadah (illustrated by Mark Podwal)

All Rivers Run to the Sea

And the Sea Is Never Full

Memoir in Two Voices (with François Mitterrand)

King Solomon and His Magic Ring (illustrated by Mark Podwal)

Conversations with Elie Wiesel (with Richard D. Heffner)

Wise Men and Their Tales

THE JUDGES

THE JUDGES

A NOVEL BY

ELIE WIESEL

SCHOCKEN BOOKS, NEW YORK

Library of Congress Cataloging-in-Publication Data
Wiesel, Elie, 1928–
[Juges. English]
The judges : a novel / Elie Wiesel.
p. cm.
Originally published: New York : Knopf, 2002.
ISBN 0-8052-1121-7
I. Title.
PQ2683.I32J8613 2004 843'.914—dc22 2004042770

www.schocken.com

Printed in the United States of America
First American Paperback
4 6 8 9 7 5 3

And in those days the judges themselves were judged.

THE MIDRASH

If the judge were just, perhaps the criminal would not be guilty.

DOSTOYEVSKY

THE JUDGES

OUTSIDE, the wolves, if there were any, must have been jubilant; they reigned supreme over a doomed world. Razziel pictured a pack of them in full cry, anticipating the delight of falling upon sleeping prey, and that reminded him dimly of the troubling landscape of his youth. Were these the only things that seemed familiar to him, his only points of reference? Was there no face he could have called to mind for reassurance? Yes, there was one: that of an old wise man, wise and mad, mad with love and daring, with thirst for life and knowledge, the ravaged face of Paritus. Whenever Razziel thought about his own past, Paritus always surfaced in his memory.

The storm was violent, driven by the fury, both blind and blinding, of a thousand wounded monsters; when would its howling cease? It seemed as if it were pitilessly bent on uprooting everything, sweeping everything away to a land dominated by white death, and that this would engulf the log cabin in which he sat in this little village hidden away somewhere in the mountains between New York and

Boston. Was it the end of the world? The end of a tale whose origins were unknown to Razziel? Was he to die before having met once more with his great protector, his guide, the messenger of his destiny? Surely not; it was just a fantasy, an illusion that arose from the nightmares buried deep in Razziel's memory, from which he himself had been barred for time beyond measure.

A strange orator roused him from his reverie. Theatrical, with a harsh, emphatic voice, he was delivering a speech as if he were onstage or standing before a gathering of learned men.

"I salute the gods who have guided you to this modest dwelling. Welcome. Warm yourselves, and may our meeting have a significance worthy of us all," said the man, smiling.

Were the five survivors, four men and one woman, too exhausted to be astonished at the solemn, not to say pompous, tone of these remarks? They did not react. Their host seemed to be relishing his role; no doubt this was one he had played in front of other travelers who had sought shelter beneath his roof on stormy nights.

They appeared content, these tourists who had become refugees; they were relieved—in good spirits, even. Their nightmare was over. In this room, which resembled a large monastic cell with bare, immaculately white walls, they had no cause to be uneasy. Quite the reverse; they felt lucky: Had they not just escaped catastrophe? After those interminable minutes of apprehension before the plane's forced landing, the universe had rediscovered its contours, its anchor. Their fear was dissipated. The elements would surely calm down. With solid ground beneath their feet, they enjoyed a sense of security here in this light, warm room with a host who gave evidence of the kindness of the human heart. He was smiling at them, a good sign. They had been fortunate to come across him. From now on all would be well. The other passengers would surely envy them when they exchanged stories, once back on the plane. For the moment they congratulated themselves on the outcome of an adventure that could have ended so badly.

"Damn it," murmured one of the travelers, a squat, morose man; he was rummaging in his pockets, searching for lost documents. No doubt he had left them on the plane.

Razziel understood his anxiety: They all lived in a world where a human being counts for less than a piece of paper. He almost proffered him a friendly word of reassurance—Don't worry; you know, in situations like this the authorities are understanding—but decided not to. He uttered a silent prayer, thanking the Lord for having taken care of him. The third man, tall, well-dressed, with a fedora, a mustache, and a red scarf around his neck, much in the style of a movie star, smiled at the woman, who was swathed in a fur coat. The danger was barely past and he was already beginning to flirt. The woman, who was put out at having left her gloves behind, blew on her fingers. Razziel glanced at the youngest of the group, who seemed indifferent to what was happening to them. This young man had something on his mind, something that was of no concern to his fellow travelers. If he was in a hurry to continue his journey, he did not show it. His eyes were focused on their host: There was something forced and false about him. His smile was disconcerting rather than reassuring. There was a fixity about his stare, a rigidity about his movements, like an actor; he seemed to be cooking up some secret plan, although his guests were not yet aware of it.

"First let us thank you for your hospitality," said the woman, an ebullient young redhead, offering him her hand, which he appeared not to see. "Truly—"

"It is I who must thank you," replied her benefactor, assisting her, with exaggerated courtesy, to remove her elegant fur coat. "If you only knew how dismal and monotonous existence can be here, especially in winter. The local people get depressed. All they can think about is the weather. And all the world does here is grow old. Sometimes we feel forgotten, both by History and by men. By the gods too. Thanks to you, things will happen. What would life be without its little surprises? I am obliged to you for the Creator's gift to man: his capacity to surprise."

Then he introduced himself.

"I am the owner of this modest house. My name would mean nothing to you; besides, it's of little significance. What's in a name? I could give you a dozen. But instead let me tell you my profession. I am a judge. And, indeed, tonight I will be *your* judge."

What a showman, Razziel said to himself, still unaware that the nightmare was beginning. How subtle this fellow is. And crafty. In putting on this performance for us, he's trying to make us forget the danger we have just escaped and help to pass the time while we wait. Only later did he realize that the real source of danger was this character himself. At this moment he seemed overly amiable and welcoming, eager to win the confidence and gratitude of his guests, which they were fully disposed to accord him.

"Please be so kind as to listen to me carefully. This little house is not exactly paradise; it does not allow me to offer you bedrooms. These are already occupied by my staff. You will be meeting my chief assistant shortly. His correct name is—oh, forget it. As he's not very tall, he prefers to be called the 'Little One,' or, as he's not very handsome, you could call him the 'Hunchback' because he's—"

"Fine. We get the picture," the young woman interrupted, laughing. "If you're not careful he might sue you for assault on his dignity."

The Judge glanced at her reprovingly. "Interrupting a judge can be a serious offense."

"Or an enjoyable sin," intervened the elegant man.

"Oh, well, sins. I know a thing or two about *them,*" said the young woman.

The Judge ignored these remarks. "This room is heated by two electric radiators, which my assistant can regulate from outside. If you are too hot or too cold, let us know. The bathroom is behind me—the narrow door there, you see? Does anyone need . . . ?"

No volunteers. In fact, Razziel would have liked to make a visit, but it was not urgent.

"When we have completed our preliminaries, an interesting task awaits us," resumed the Judge, rubbing his hands as if to warm them. "You will see. I have everything ready: pens, notebooks . . . and even some good strong tea—or is there anyone among you who would prefer coffee? I have that too. I have all you need. While you are in my house you will have nothing to complain of." A silence. "Afterward—well, afterward is another story."

The room was pleasant, furnished with simplicity: chairs

around a circular table, a sofa, dictionaries in a corner on the floor. The dandy was the first of the men to remove his overcoat, which earned him mildly ironic congratulations from the Judge: "Well done, sir. I can see you make yourself at home wherever you go."

The Judge, in his turn, removed his heavy fur-lined cape, that of a shepherd or mountain dweller. Razziel was expecting to see the man casually dressed. But he was dressed in a dark gray suit, white shirt, navy-blue tie. Very smart. As if he had just come from a dinner in town. In an indefinable way he compelled respect. Everything he said and did was calculated. If Razziel, disconcerted by the fixity of his stare, had had to guess his profession or vocation, he would have opted for undertaker in a superior funeral parlor, Protestant minister, or professor of canon law.

"So. Please be seated. Look, take this chair, it's quite comfortable. They all are. And you, madam, that one over there. You other gentlemen, take any chair. You must be exhausted. I shall remain standing."

He waited for everyone to be seated before continuing.

"Everything all right?"

Yes, everything was all right.

"If anyone wishes to change places I have no objection."

No, no one wanted to do so.

"Good. In that case, let us begin. You know who I am—that is to say, I have disclosed my profession to you. Now it is your turn. After all, we are going to spend this long night together, and perhaps others too. It's only natural, don't you agree, for all of us to introduce ourselves?"

Yes, they agreed. Oddly enough, the Judge was right.

The five survivors did not know one another. Thrown together by chance, first in the same airplane, now in this place, why should they not explain their reasons for traveling? Five lives, five stories had come together in a strange convergence. After all, any one of the Judge's "guests" could have been elsewhere; any one of them could have changed schedules or arrived too late for boarding.

"To begin with," the Judge continued, starting to pace around the table, "let us limit ourselves to basic biographical details: surname and forename, profession, place of birth, marital status, purpose of travel. Imagine you're checking in at a hotel. Making a passport or visa application. So? Who will speak first?"

The five visitors stared at him, bewildered. Was he serious? He guessed what they were thinking and added, "Let us say that this is a game, a parlor game that . . . that later, if heaven wills it, might become seriously interesting."

His "guests" were beginning to show irritation: What had they walked into? Who did he think he was, this apprentice demagogue, so abusing the situation as to make them talk about their private lives? Who authorized him to give orders? The young woman was the first to pull herself together.

"This is quite out of order, sir. I don't mind joining your game but on the condition that everyone sticks to the rules. And you too. Don't expect a special dispensation. The fact that this is your house gives you no rights over the rest of us. You wish to know us better? Very well. But we, too, would like to know *you* a little better."

"Haven't I told you who I am?"

"You're a judge. Fine. But where do you sit? What cases do you try? What school did you attend? Are you married? A father? How many children?"

The Judge looked surprised. He coughed and adopted an unexpectedly grave tone.

"Your argument, madam, seems to me irrefutable. Let us say that my name is Charles Clareman, Peter Pavlikov, or Denis Darwin. I am forty-six or sixty-four. Twice divorced—or maybe ten times. I now live alone. What else? Born in a delightful suburb of San Francisco. The son of a minister of religion. My father was a saint, my mother a whore. Appointed to my post by a higher authority, I preside over a somewhat special court. I will relieve you of the obligation to address me as Your Honor. *Judge* will suffice."

Had he expected that his comments would provoke exclamations of amusement from his guests? In fact, only the woman smiled. Razziel simply gave a start. Then his neighbor in the red scarf burst out laughing, slapping his knee.

"That's wonderful, that's great, Your Honor!" And, half getting up, added, "You're not serious."

The Judge made a gesture with both his hands, as if to say, Who knows? Maybe I am, maybe I'm not.

An indefinable unease overcame Razziel. He thought of his old Master; he too had had many names and many ages. If this was a game, it was going to be played out at the very edges of reality.

"Please fill out these questionnaires," said the Judge, in softer tones and a more sober voice. "After the formalities I will take care of the hot drinks."

"Why not right away?" asked the young woman.

"It takes time to prepare them. I suggest you get to work."

"You're joking!" exclaimed the man in the red scarf. "Maybe you'd like to check our passports as well?"

The Judge seemed slightly irritated. "Why not? It's a good idea. We'll see, after."

"After what?"

"After the formalities."

The redhead shrugged her shoulders in resignation: What was the point of arguing with this madman? Motionless, the youngest member of the group observed the scene without becoming involved.

The Judge took a sheet of paper out of his pocket and said, "With your permission, I will read you the document filled out in his time by the Hunchback. It might serve as an example."

Let us praise the Judge. Let him be praised by those who know him and by those who shall come to know him. Let him be praised by the heavens and the angels who dwell there. Let him be praised by the gods, for they are good.

As for me, I am young, or maybe old, I no longer know. I don't even know if I am myself, if the man addressing you is indeed me. The Judge knows. He knows everything.

From the beginning the Judge has been my whole universe and the sun that shines upon it. I would climb all the trees on earth, swallow every drop of dew, kill everything that breathes just to see him smile. Do I not owe my life to him? What was I for him? A human puppet for him to play with? A buffoon sent by the gods in a bout of good (or bad) temper? A disciple, whose twisted body resembled his own soul? I was scarcely ten years old when I came to his home. I had lost everything in an accident. The Judge is my only living link with my childhood. Did my parents have brothers, sisters, cousins? They never mentioned them. And so the Judge became my father, my uncle, my friend, and my enemy. Sometimes I told myself that it was for me that he invented all his "games," more for my enlightenment than for his own. To teach me what it was to be a man.

Unhappily, I was human but not a man.

The Judge folded the sheet of paper and put it back in his pocket.

"Now you must admit there's a text fit for an anthology! Let's see which one of you can match it."

The woman made a face. "Oh, no! I feel as if I were back in high school . . . in a religious-education class. My poor literature teacher; he despaired of me. . . . My homework was always hopeless unless I copied from a friend. . . . I hope you're going to be more tolerant."

The Judge, his hand on his brow as if to concentrate better, gave her a hard look. He was on the brink of reprimanding her, changed his mind, and said nothing. Bravo, thought the impassive young man. Well done. It was time someone put him in his place, this odd fellow with his superior airs, who thinks he's . . . who *does* he think he is? It doesn't matter. What matters is that he's met his match.

The four men studied the young woman with growing interest. Despite her fatigue she remained in perfect command of herself—arched back, sensual mouth, somewhat masculine face, dark eyes marked by memories both sweet and stormy, no trace of makeup on her face. Here was a woman who could stand up for herself: a fighter. No doubt dangerous when she was angry. The man in the red scarf found her interesting. Pretty, even.

She hesitated before mumbling, "Oh, well, it's better than freezing outside," and began writing reluctantly, keeping her head held high.

> Everyone calls me Claudia. Age unspecified. Well, let's say, thirty-something. Married? No: divorced. No children. Profession: press agent for a theater company. Purpose of travel? None of your business.

Her neighbor, the man who looked as if he had lost his papers, wrote studiously, licking his lips with his tongue.

> George Kirsten. Age: forty-two. Born in Düsseldorf. Married. The father of two children. Profession: archivist. Purpose of travel?

George hesitated for a moment. Should he tell the truth? He chose not to.

> Meeting with European and Israeli colleagues to prepare for an international congress on the value and ambiguity of oral testimony.

Bruce Schwarz took out his gold pen and, with an expression of contempt, dashed off a few words and sat up triumphantly.

I'm writing this because I choose to do so. I also suggest that you go to hell. My life is mine and mine alone. That goes for my past too. Born yesterday, but old enough to know all I need to know about existence. I always have a fiancée but I remain a bachelor; my aim is to enjoy life to the fullest. They call me a playboy. It's an occupation like any other, and has the added advantage that fixed places of work and residence are not required. Purpose of travel: to meet up with lady friends. I hope you have no objection!

Razziel simply noted:

Razziel Friedman. Originally from Central Europe. Age uncertain. Parents unknown. Profession: principal of a Talmudic school. Purpose of travel: to meet a man who says he knows me better than I know myself. And he's probably the only person in the world who could make this claim.

The youngest of the travelers, his hands in his pockets, appeared to be bored. Detached from what was happening around him, he had not touched the pen and paper set before him.

"How about you?" the Judge addressed him. "Are you dreaming? You have your head in the clouds. Do you have nothing to tell us?"

"I have no desire to say anything."

The Judge's tone hardened abruptly. "Sometimes one does things even without desire."

"Not me."

"And suppose I said you were being antisocial and in that case you have no place here?"

"Say it."

"And suppose I turned you out?"

"Are you threatening me?"

The Judge stared at him for a long while, almost lost his temper, but only grumbled: "There's a time for everything."

Claudia judged this an opportune moment to intervene in order to dissipate the tension. "Do it for us, young man. Not for him. I'm asking you . . . very nicely."

The young man smiled faintly. "You shouldn't act as a spokesperson for someone who's trying to impose his will on you."

Now it was George's turn to join the argument. Dressed in a winter suit with frayed sleeves, he spoke in a drawling voice; everything about him was ponderous.

"But, you see, it's not like that at all," he said, trying to calm tempers. "The Judge isn't our jailer, you know. He's our benefactor! Isn't he entitled to our trust, if not our gratitude?"

"Don't you think," said Claudia, "as a gesture . . . ?"

"And one that commits you to nothing," said Bruce. "I'm just as stubborn as you are, but do what I've done. Don't be a killjoy. Put down a few words on your goddamned paper so we can all get to drink the tea we've so graciously been offered."

"No."

"That's absurd," said George.

"What are you trying to prove?" asked Claudia.

"That I'm a free man."

Obstinately the young man maintained his refusal. But faced with the insistence of his fellow hostages, he agreed to make an oral statement.

"My name is Yoav. Born in Jerusalem. I'm a reserve officer in the army."

"So you're an Israeli!" exclaimed Claudia. "That explains everything, my dear Yoav." The very mention of Israel seemed to delight her. "What a beautiful name!" she went on. "What a great people! Isn't Israel famous for her inflexible pride?" And, turning to the Judge: "Are you satisfied with that information?"

The Judge replied that, yes, he was satisfied. He stopped striding up and down the room, gathered up the sheets of paper, looked over them, and pronounced, "Naturally, this is only a beginning: an overture, let us say. Act one will come later. But first I shall bring you some hot drinks."

I was mistaken, thought Razziel. He's neither an undertaker nor a professor of law. He's just a plain old schoolteacher. A schoolteacher with no pupils.

The Judge looked at his wristwatch, murmured "It's still early," put the four sheets of paper into a folder, and went out.

First there was silence, then the chatter began again. Fuller introductions, comments, polite exchanges.

"He's a real pain," said Claudia, getting up to restore her circulation. "I wish he'd come in again soon and take us back to the plane. Perhaps we can get tea somewhere else."

Everyone agreed.

Through the window they could see a moonless night riven by furious winds.

The weather forecast the previous day had predicted snow but not this avalanche. At Kennedy Airport the majority of the flights had left on time, or almost. Universal Air (Flight 420 New York to Tel Aviv) had taken off about ten minutes late because the cabin crew was not complete: One hostess was missing, caught in a traffic jam on the Triboro Bridge. Pnina, her replacement, kept apologizing to the passengers on behalf of her colleague. The captain, who was in good humor, laid it on thick. "You see, ladies and gentlemen, when the lady you're waiting for doesn't show up, the replacement is always better."

Several feminists among the passengers grumbled a bit.

"It's OK by me, God watches over us," Pnina, who was Jewish, jokingly whispered to a colleague. "There are lots of Jews on this flight. Look at them. They're praying. I wonder what for. Husbands for their middle-aged daughters? I hope they'll leave one for me, I too could use a husband."

"Let them pray, they're not doing anyone any harm."

"Do you think they have no faith in us?"

"What does it matter? With their prayers and our pilots' skills, we'll be just fine."

The flight attendant was right. There were a lot of Jews on board. The plane that evening was reminiscent of a synagogue. Dotted here and there among the rows of seats, many of the passengers were reciting from the Psalms in anticipation of celebrating Hanukkah, the feast of lights, the following day. With God's help, in less than twenty-four hours they would be in Jerusalem to light the first candle.

At about 10 P.M. the plane wrenched itself up from the earth with a violent heave. Down below, countless little lights were winking away, as if sending messages in code. The atmosphere was charged with anticipation and exuberance. A mother kissed her baby. An old man patted a little boy's head and whispered to him something the boy did not understand. To the right of him a man of indeterminate age stifled a yawn.

The captain made the usual announcement: "We have just left Kennedy Airport. The flight will be ten hours, thirty-two minutes. We will be flying at a height of thirty thousand feet, and we expect to encounter some zones of turbulence. But you will sleep well. When you wake, you'll see the sun shining over the Holy Land." There was applause. The plane reached its cruising altitude, and the flight attendants began serving drinks at the front. Razziel was in seat 10 C—the tenth row, on the aisle. In three minutes' time he would be drinking his coffee. No, he wouldn't. The captain announced, "We're experiencing some turbulence now, ladies and gentlemen. In view of the wind speed, please return to your seats and fasten your seat belts."

Suddenly everything began to move. The beverage cart began sliding in all directions. Those who had been lucky enough to get drinks now regretted it; they were drenched. They laughed: Tomorrow it would all be forgotten.

And what was Razziel thinking about? The man who held the key to his secret past. When was it they had first met? It was back there, in prison, in the cell. Razziel had told him about all the ordeals he had endured, in that baleful laboratory where doctors played games with his memory, as if it were a film from which unwanted outtakes ended up in the trash can. Paritus, my savior. What would have become of me without you?

Now Paritus awaited him in Israel. It was in order to see him again that Razziel was making this journey. Thank you, Paritus, you kept your word, thank you, for you will help me piece together the fragments of my broken life.

The five survivors had not been sitting together on the plane. Before the turbulence began, Claudia had been asleep. Bruce had been trying to flirt with a flight attendant. George was reading a scientific journal. Yoav was vaguely listening to the chatter of his neighbors. And Razziel was letting his mind wander. The weather was stormy? Less dramatic than the storms of the human soul, and less disturbing. As for Pnina, she was checking that the pilot's instructions were being observed.

Suddenly the plane plunged into an air pocket—then into another, deeper one. Claudia woke with a start. Breathless, Bruce thought he was going to faint. Yoav gripped his seat with both hands so hard it hurt. As often in the past few months, he thought about death: Can one die without suffering? And to think that, while in uniform, he had escaped death so often. How ironic it would be to encounter it now! Someone cried out, "The engine! The engine! Listen to the sound it's making!" The cabin was filled with shouting; some passengers had suffered head wounds. The flight attendants strove to restore calm. A Hasid with a flowing beard, his right hand over his eyes, murmured the Shma. A woman shouted "Help!" A little boy wept; Pnina knelt down and dried his tears. Razziel's neighbor was muttering, "I don't believe in God, but I hope he won't let us down."

A voice said, "I'm a doctor." The captain asked everyone to remain seated. A moment later the doctor was asked to lend a hand. He hurried to the rear of the aircraft where an old man was groaning, shaken by spasms. Heart attack? Cerebral hemorrhage? The plane began bucking again. The intercom was silent. People were asking the flight attendants, "What's going on? Is anybody injured? What's going to happen to us?"

"Nothing. Nothing serious. Keep your seat belts fastened." To calm the passengers, Pnina explained, "It's just a bad patch; in another minute we'll have left the turbulence behind."

The captain came on the intercom. "Nothing has happened to the plane; it has sustained no damage. But since there's a storm brewing, I think it best for us to land somewhere. It's impossible for us to go back to Kennedy, but we're in contact with several air traffic control towers. Most of the major airports in the area are closed. Boston still has one runway open. . . . Damn, they've just closed it." The passengers held their breath. Several Hasidim were now reciting prayers in Hebrew, echoed in English by a Christian woman. The old man with the heart attack had calmed down. His terrified grandson held his hand.

George Kirsten reviewed the situation: If he were to die now he would be free at last, and so would his wife. But Pamela? She would still have her job at the National Archives and would certainly find a way to fill her evenings. But the children? What would happen to them?

Claudia was thinking about the man in her life, her life restored at last: Who would tell him what only she could reveal? At that moment David was so present to her that she had to make an effort not to burst into tears.

Yoav reflected that if something happened to the pilot he could take his place. So maybe his experience in the air force would be of some use.

Razziel was wondering if Paritus might not also be on a plane, buffeted by tempestuous winds like this one, in which case their meeting might never take place. Suddenly he saw Paritus again: his slow reassuring gestures, his learning, immense yet flexible, his promises—

The captain's voice: "Good news. There's a small airfield close by, in Connecticut. We're going to land there in a few moments. Keep smiling. Things are looking up."

There follow interminable moments of tension, meditation, and anguished hope; regret too. "I shouldn't have come. . . . I should have waited for a better forecast." If only man could undo what he does.

Too late for regrets. At any rate, the end of the ordeal is approaching. The pilot makes the best landing of his career. Despite poor visibility and damaged radar, the plane touches down, glides along the snow-covered runway for a few seconds, and comes to a halt just before a barbed-wire fence. The fear is gone; the passengers salute the pilot with a thunder of applause and cheering; he thanks them. "What did I tell you? These modern airplanes are strong enough to withstand the worst storms. Everything is ready for your temporary stay here. As soon as weather permits, we will reassemble to continue our flight."

The pilot is an optimist. Does he not know the old saying, "Man proposes and God disposes"? In Yiddish they say, "Man acts and God laughs."

The airfield is deserted. There is only one light, the flashlight belonging to the watchman. Muffled from head to toe, he helps the passengers deplane. He murmurs, "You've been lucky, really lucky. . . . It's a miracle, a real miracle." With the help of the crew he leads them to a kind of barn, empty and ice cold: the waiting room. "I'll make a few calls to the villagers." Half an hour later, cars equipped with snow gear arrive. A dozen men have responded to the appeal. Each will take as many passengers as possible.

"It's just a matter of a few hours," says the pilot. "Tomorrow morning we'll continue the flight." The watchman and the crew arrange the allocation of sleeping quarters. Families and friends are not split up. For the others it is a lottery; mere chance determines Razziel's group. Their car is the seventh.

The Hunchback appeared with the tea. Short, stocky, with a hairy, disfigured face and unevenly arched shoulders—everything about him, including his rapid movements, was disturbing. He belonged to another world, another species. Claudia offered to pour the tea, but the Hunchback refused.

"You are our guests, after all," he said, in a surprisingly melodious voice. And, with a little sarcastic laugh, "What would History say if we failed in our obligations?"

Razziel concealed his astonishment: What did History have to do with them? Wasn't History busy elsewhere with a more important cast of characters? He attributed this remark to a bizarre form of irony on the part of the Hunchback. Perhaps he was trying to imitate his master.

"Who takes sugar?"

"I don't suppose you have a lemon in this fine restaurant?" said Claudia, in a tone intended to be relaxed and amused.

"We apologize, but the supermarket was closed today," the Hunchback replied, making a gesture of contrition. "It's the snow, you know. . . . We deeply regret it and ask your indulgence."

He went out backward, spinning the empty tray that he held in one hand and leaving his guests to sip their scalding-hot tea in peace. Did they suspect that their fortunes were soon to take a turn for the worse? In the muted light they started chatting again.

"All that ugliness concentrated in one body makes me uneasy," Bruce remarked.

"As much as the Judge does?" asked Razziel.

The intuition he had inherited from his parents and also from his people had led him to be wary of the Judge from the very first moment. Was it his sly exaggerated courtesy? The icy glints flashing through his rigid gaze? This was a person who awakened in him memories that had long been buried.

"Yes," replied Bruce. "As much as the Judge."

"I don't share your reaction," said Razziel.

"Why not?"

"The Hunchback doesn't lie; his outward shape reflects his inner nature. That's not true of the Judge. I don't know why, but I am suspect of every single thing he says. In fact, I think he holds the whole world in contempt. And he's not a judge; he knows nothing about the law and does not preside over any court worthy of the name."

"But in that case," said Claudia, "how do you explain the warmth and humanity of his welcome? That was sincere. Otherwise why would he have come out of his house to take us in and offer us shelter and food?"

"I can't explain it," Razziel admitted, "but my experience tells me that certain things, certain events, seem inexplicable only for a time: up to the moment when the veil is torn aside."

Claudia studied him. "I'm less of a pessimist than you. Your mistrust surprises me. What do you have against the Judge? He seems very considerate. Friendly. Happy to know we're safe and sound. Why would he lie to us?"

"Perhaps he has his reasons," said Razziel.

Bruce concurred with Claudia's opinion. George and Yoav seemed detached from the discussion, as if it did not concern them.

"All the same, I'd like to be gone from here, right now," George finally admitted, scratching the bald spot on his head.

"Me too," said Claudia.

For diverse reasons they were all impatient to reach Israel.

"I'm afraid it won't be for quite a while," Razziel said. "Who knows when the storm will abate? And whether the plane will be in a state to take off."

"We're not there yet," agreed Bruce.

"What a waste of time!" Claudia burst out. "With all the urgent matters waiting for me in Tel Aviv."

At that, Bruce lost his temper. His voice shot out

angrily from between his fleshy lips. "You're not the only one!"

"If that's your approach to seducing women, you're not doing well."

"Seduce you? I pity the man in your life. An affair with you wouldn't be much fun."

"How dare you!"

George intervened. "Calm down, please. This is not a time to squabble. If we carry on like this we'll end up finding one another intolerable. You know as well as I do what history teaches us: It's easy enough to start a quarrel, but it's much harder to end it."

"Mind your own business," Bruce answered, raising his voice. "I'll say what I like."

Yoav finally felt the need to break his silence. "Please, spare your nerves! You will probably need them. All of us are understandably tense—but here we are, condemned to spend these few hours in one another's company. This calls for a little civility and restraint."

Claudia abruptly changed color; the Israeli officer's voice had made her think of David. Maybe they knew one another. In Israel, people said, everyone knows everyone. Isn't it more like one big family, rather than a country?

"You're a soldier by profession but you speak like a born diplomat," she remarked, smiling.

"When children quarrel, an adult needs to intervene," explained Yoav, returning her smile.

"Now that's the last straw!" shouted Bruce.

Fortunately, just then the door opened. Razziel felt a chill and shivered. The Judge entered and seated himself at the end of the table.

"I declare this hearing open," he said solemnly.

Claudia burst out laughing.

"I should like to know what you find so amusing," muttered Bruce, adjusting the scarf around his neck.

She was about to say it was no concern of his, but the Judge spoke first.

"For the time being you are all free. Free to laugh or to daydream. To live or to forget you are alive. After, we shall see."

"After what?" demanded Bruce.

"A little patience would not come amiss, Mr. Schwarz. Everything in its proper time."

"May we smoke?" asked Claudia.

"Can't you restrain yourself?" asked George. "Smoking in a confined space is hardly what any doctor would recommend to people who care about their health."

"Any other views?" asked the Judge.

Bruce was in favor of smoking and Razziel against. Razziel thought about Kali and her accursed cancer. Kali had never stopped smoking.

The Judge considered the issue for a moment and delivered a verdict without appeal. "You may smoke."

Loftily Claudia lit her cigarette, drew on it several times, and stubbed it out in the saucer in front of her.

"Thank you," said George.

The Judge glared at him. "Now let us speak of serious matters."

"OK," said Bruce. "What's the weather forecast? How long do you think we'll be enjoying your hospitality? Does the crew know where we are? So that when—"

He did not finish his sentence, but a gesture of his hand sufficed to express his meaning.

"Is that all?" asked the Judge.

"Yes. For the moment."

The Judge stiffened before continuing. "You speak as if your friends had chosen you as official spokesman. If that is the case you must inform me."

"Holy smoke, you're crazy!"

"Take care how you address the court. Contempt of court is a serious offense! I asked you a question. Please give me your answer."

"OK. The answer is negative. But as for my questions—they were *my* questions, and I should like you to answer them."

The Judge stared at him fiercely. "The news is not encouraging. The forecast is relatively pessimistic, I'm sorry to say. The weather is not expected to clear tonight. Or tomorrow."

"What are we going to do?" yelled Bruce, standing up abruptly.

"Wait," said the Judge, stroking his brow as if to erase a doubt. His voice became harsh. "Sit down!"

"I have no desire to sit."

"I order you to sit down," repeated the Judge. There was a hint of a threat in his hoarse voice.

Four pairs of eyes watched a confrontation from which the Judge emerged the victor. His calm was stronger than Bruce's anger. The latter finally obeyed.

"I'd like to make a telephone call," said Claudia.

Bruce echoed her. "Me too."

"It's essential for me to notify someone of what's happened to us," explained Claudia.

Me too, I should be warning someone who's waiting for me, thought Razziel. I totally depend on him. But how can I reach him? Actually, he should know how to find me. Like in the old days. He always knew where I was heading and why. He knew things about me that I'm still unaware of.

"The people expecting you are doubtless informed about what's going on. This storm will be headline news in all the papers."

"I still need to make a call," said Claudia.

"I am afraid that is impossible. The lines are down. The telephone is dead. Not only mine; everybody else's too. Practically speaking, we are isolated, cut off from the outside world."

Bruce banged his fist on the table, making the cups and saucers dance. "What a mess! Why did we have to land in this filthy little hole? Why did I take that flight? What have I ever done to God that I should end up with this idiot?"

Claudia tried to calm him.

"Why get annoyed? Instead of insulting this village and our kind host, you'd do better to thank him for having taken us in."

There was no love lost between the playboy and the young redhead, that much was plain. Temperamentally they seemed bound to clash; the two of them were seething. Too bad for them, thought Razziel. They'll end up exhausting themselves.

Neither more nor less interested than before, a scrupulous and neutral examiner, his right index finger in his vest, the Judge was observing them, sizing up each word, each intonation, as if to probe them, to compare them with the reactions of other people he had had in his power, whether long ago or only yesterday. His voice, full of authority, called them to order.

"I have studied your biographical notes. Since we have some time ahead of us, I propose to go into them in more detail."

No, thought Razziel, he's neither an undertaker nor a priest. He seems to think he's a police chief or a desk officer; he's read too much Kafka or Borges.

"There are questions here that it behooves us to clarify. What has brought you together under my roof, mere chance? That would be too facile a conclusion. I don't believe it. Behind mere chance there must be something else. A design? A conspiracy? A strategy conceived by some higher power? Which one, God? That too is too facile. Who is hiding behind him?"

"Don't you think you're taking things a bit too far?" cried Bruce, showing off.

"Don't you see our host is being theatrical?" Claudia reprimanded him. "Let him have his fun."

It's true, thought Razziel, he thinks he's onstage. But what role is he playing? These biographical statements extorted from us, these ridiculous interrogations, what is their point? And how can one explain the ominous sense of disquiet that has been growing ever since we set foot in this house?

"I must ask both of you not to interrupt me," said the Judge, without looking up.

And so the mechanism was triggered for a sequence of events that provoked in each of the participants first incredulity, then panic, as at the approach of some catastrophe.

Alone in a room next door from which he could observe the five travelers, the Hunchback reflected on his own situation, referring to himself, the Judge's servant, his slave, as if to a stranger.

Some beings are watched over by God, others are watched by a man who believes he is the emissary of Death and the embodiment of its derision. But why does this man need a slave at his side?

Who shall live? Who shall die? Who shall judge the Judge?

For the moment everything is still possible. But at what stage does a man become the hostage of someone he believes to be his savior? This woman, still young; will she catch Fate's eye? And why has the slave fallen in love with her? If she will only love me, *he says to himself,* I will take the place of the Lord and cure men of the ills that overcome them. *Did he utter these words out loud or only in his head? He cannot recall. But the fact is that for a variety of reasons he does not dare intervene, at least not right away. Perhaps he hesitates to reveal the truth about the man who holds him shackled. For during the many years he has lived in this man's shadow he has learned things about his master that still, today, leave him perplexed and filled with doubt.*

What are these forces that the Judge seeks to tame or to

defy? Guardian angel one day and tempter the next, he delights in inspiring fear. Fear is the meaning he gives to his own life. But just to his life?

And the wretched slave who despairs of his liberty, what meaning does his *life have? When did he discover himself capable of love? Just a moment ago, as he secretly watched that still-youthful woman whose lower lip has started to tremble.*

It was the first time he had felt such an emotion in the presence of a woman—no, his mother had inspired it in him too. As soon as he caught sight of her, he would run to meet her, sweating, his heart beating fit to burst, ready to give his life for a caress. But that was in the old days, before the accident. Since then women (even the pharmacist's wife) have left him indifferent, cold; compared to his mother, they seemed pale, distant. But not this evening. The red-haired woman: He had stared at her open-mouthed, his throat constricted, gasping for breath. Why do people call this a coup de foudre*? He would prefer words like* illumination *or* vision.

It had seemed to him as if the young woman were addressing him in a murmur. Was it a prayer? A cry for help? Or was she simply talking to herself, seeking to understand what was happening to her?

It's for you to judge; it's your move, the Hunchback tells himself.

PAST MIDNIGHT.

Is the snow going to swallow up the whole world? And finally even time itself?

Snow is like money, or like love. Some people use it for their amusement, even to cleanse themselves; others become tainted by it. Children play with it, as do sportsmen. Snowballs, snowmen, victories on the snow, gold medals and world fame.

And yet. . . .

As he studied the documents on the table, the Judge was talking to himself. "Who to begin with? Why not Mr. Schwarz? Since he's so talkative, perhaps he can enlighten us about the anger he seems to be bursting with."

And he began to interrogate Bruce, as if he had been held for questioning or even charged: Why did he adopt such a coarse, perverse, and hostile manner? Was it his intention to challenge the authority of the court and its president? As for his profession, why did he make such a mystery of it? He claimed to be a playboy. What exactly did that mean? A spoiled child? A "boy" who seeks only pleasure and enjoyment in life? A gigolo, perhaps? Is this a way for a decent man to make a living? Is it an ideal to be celebrated and taught?

The Judge asked these questions in a neutral professional monotone. Even as he accused Bruce of refusing to abide by the Law, he raised it as a technicality, speaking in sober tones, devoid of all personal animosity. He was simply doing his job as a judge, his duty as a citizen, conscious of his obligations. If the accused persisted in sabotaging the investigation, too bad for him. "Sabotaging" was possibly an extreme word, but the said Bruce Schwarz was doing nothing to facilitate the Judge's task, and this made him all the more suspect. He simply responded to every question with an insult or an evasive gesture. Sometimes the Judge was obliged to repeat himself in the same harsh, dry voice, as if to emphasize the seriousness of the matter, which irritated Bruce but no more than that. It was only when the Judge came to his relationships with women that he burst into loud laughter.

"Aha! Now we're coming to it, you dirty little pervert! Porn stories, that's what you want, isn't it? So you want to be aroused, you dirty little skunk, is that it?"

Without responding to these personal attacks, the Judge waited for him to calm down before continuing his interrogation, which proved quite fruitless.

Maybe because she wanted to distance herself from her fellow traveler, Claudia adopted a more conciliatory, almost friendly, attitude.

"Parlor games can sometimes be a useful distraction. What can I contribute?"

"You describe yourself as a press agent. You work for a theater. Which one?"

"A small company but one with a good reputation. Off-Broadway, of course."

"What's it called?"

"The Stage Mirror. It's a charming little auditorium. It seats four hundred. It's intimate and cozy. Experimental. The actors are all very young, like their audience; they are very young too."

"What is playing there right now?"

"A first play by a blind writer. The parents of the hero—who is blind—have given him an unreal picture of the world, so he won't feel deprived of its riches. But his fiancée won't be a party to this deception. She loves him and believes her love should be enough for him. He has to choose."

A brief argument ensued. Casting himself in the role of theater critic, Bruce pronounced the plot too abstract. With some irony, Claudia offered him a lesson in dramatic theory: It all depends on the performers, she said. Some actors can recite a page from the telephone directory and make an audience laugh or weep. "Last year," she recalled, "our company created an original drama, a monologue. Believing himself to be dead in the midst of a healthy society, the character upsets everybody. At a certain moment he stares at the audience with his demented eyes and cries out, 'In a novel by Axel Munthe, the great Swedish writer who adored kings and birds, a man declares that he is dead but does not know it. Well, I am dead and I *do* know it. You are the ones who don't know it. That's why you don't understand me. You're afraid, afraid of understanding the dead. . . .' I just wish I could describe the shudder that ran through the audience."

She spoke so passionately that no one dared to interrupt her. Razziel congratulated her. Bruce, clearly miffed, snorted. Yoav was miles away. George smiled.

"What's your opinion, George?" asked the Judge.

"I rarely go to the theater."

"Never?"

"Rarely."

"So you don't care for the theater?"

"Not at all. It's just that I live in a world in which only the written or printed word exists. Words have their own secrets, which I try to fathom without harming them. Sometimes I see them dancing or catching fire. That's when I really come alive."

The Judge repeated his last words in cold tones: "That's how you really come alive. Hmm." Suddenly irritated, he turned to Yoav, still as distracted as ever. "And how about you, general, what do you think?"

Yoav did not reply at once.

"I asked what you are thinking about."

"About the first play that was mentioned. I've seen blind men in my war-torn country often enough. Soldiers with damaged eyes. Tank crews who miraculously escaped from their burning tanks, their bodies half burned, their eyelids torn off."

"What do you think of Claudia's play?"

"Hold it! Let's not get carried away," exclaimed Claudia. "I didn't write it."

"I don't know the play," said Yoav. "All I know is I won't go to see it."

"Why not?"

"I have no desire to watch seeing actors pretending to be blind."

"How about you, Razziel?"

"In the school of which I'm the principal, the theater is not a subject of study. Unlike ancient Greece, in the world of the Talmud the theater doesn't exist."

"But the theme of the blind man?"

"I find blind people fascinating. They see a world that is not mine. But one world interests me as much as the other."

"Mr. Kirsten? What does the archivist think of this debate?"

George smiled. Should he reply that he found Claudia attractive? She reminded him of a younger Pamela, though she did not look like her. Everything about her pleased him: the way she held herself, the way she expressed herself, her ironic manner toward the playboy, her deep breathing, her half-open lips. She was the type of woman he liked to be attracted to. Like Pamela.

"I imagine that in the theater all subjects are good," he said.

"Coward," said Bruce.

"Diplomat," corrected Claudia.

She winked at George; they were accomplices now. They shared a secret that had just been born but as yet had no name—or future. Was it because she seemed to have sensed his vulnerability and decided to protect him? Or was her smile for all those who fell under the spell of theater?

"Mr. Kirsten!" said the Judge.

George did not react. Was he daydreaming?

"Mr. Kirsten! I am addressing you. I am speaking to you, and you are not listening. Does what we are engaged in here not interest you?"

"Excuse me. The journey has exhausted me. I don't seem able to concentrate."

The Judge pretended to consult his papers. "Your biographical notice is somewhat brief."

"That's inevitable; there's nothing special about my life."

"You're an archivist."

"Yes."

"What are you looking for in your archives?"

George blinked; he did not understand the question. It was the first time anyone had put it to him. What can an archivist look for in the documents under his care, precise answers to vague questions? The truth of man's attraction to lies? The secrets of the genetic code? The origins of time? This line of questioning irritated him.

"Long ago," he said finally, "I dreamed of becoming a scientist. But that's a very special area where sometimes what you find is the thing you *weren't* looking for. Luckily, I didn't have an aptitude for science. So I turned to the study of archives. There, you do know what you're looking for and how to find it."

"All that is very interesting, but you have not answered my question. What are *you* looking for in your archives? What do you seek to conserve?"

George thought deeply. "Memory," he said.

"Whose?"

"That of the dead and that of the living."

"In other words," Razziel intervened, "your ambition is to be the memory of memory."

George's thoughtful look reflected a mixture of surprise and gratitude.

"Wonderful!" exclaimed Claudia. "For me, memory evokes the theater. For what is a performance if not a fragment of memory in the art of being born? It lives only for an instant in eternity, a powerful human appeal to the beauty of an existence that is nevertheless inevitably committed to the ugliness and decrepitude of death."

"Nonsense!" remarked Bruce, just to annoy her.

Their conversation sounded, for the moment, like a debate between intellectuals on a café terrace on a summer's day or around an open fire on a winter's evening.

"That's enough, all of you!" the Judge declared. "We're not here to listen to your rhetorical debates."

"But why *are* we here?" asked Claudia innocently.

"You will learn in due course."

All of them still believed this was a harmless whim on the part of their host: He was amusing himself by amusing them. To pass the time. To make their waiting more tolerable. Perhaps it was his way of offering his guests a little entertainment.

The Judge turned to George. "You are very quiet, too quiet. What lies behind your silence?"

"Perhaps another silence."

"I don't understand."

"It's difficult to explain. I prefer written material. When I have to speak, I imagine I'm reading. In silence."

"Is it asking too much of you to make an effort?"

When George said nothing, Razziel came to the rescue.

"With your permission, I believe I understand. . . . How can I put it? People are mistaken if they believe that the only choice is between silence and speech. One silence can hide another. In a moment of grace sometimes we are able to lift one of these layers of silence. But at once others arise and confuse us."

"And what of the present?" the Judge persisted. "Does it have no importance for you, Mr. Archivist?"

"No. I feel its impact but I try to resist it."

"In other words, only the past attracts you. What about your own contemporaries? Don't they exist for you?"

"Yesterday I helped a painter finish his canvas."

"And the day before yesterday?"

"The day before yesterday I told stories to an old man who was afraid of dying."

"And the day before that?"

"I listened to the singing of a woman in love."

The Judge is dangerous, George thought. How can I put him off the scent? He did not know why, but he knew it was essential to hide from him the burden that weighed on him, the secret document on which depended a man's future—and perhaps his very life.

"So far we have been speaking about words and, above all, about silence," said the Judge, fixing him with a cold stare. "One day I would like to be able to consult your archives. Is there one in which silence is preserved? Let us say: the silence of memory?"

George had a moment of alarm—am I going to be able

to deceive him?—but managed a smile, in which pride and sorrow were mingled, and remained silent. Once again, Razziel decided to speak for him.

"If you will allow me, Your Honor. In reply I should say that silence can certainly be found in archives. The memory of silence is something we crave and seek. But as for the silence of memory—that, never."

This was when George chose to display his erudition. He devoted five minutes to explaining the importance of archives, the way they sustain the culture of mankind and its civilization. Without them, justice, for example, would be an empty word.

Surprised by his eloquence, Claudia could not help remarking with some warmth, "My goodness! For someone who deals in silence you certainly can be eloquent."

Razziel couldn't explain it to himself, but he felt a pang of jealousy; Claudia was showing herself to be too well disposed, almost admiring, toward this somber, balding archivist spewing platitudes. Then a flush of shame rose to his cheeks.

Meanwhile, the Judge was staring curiously at Yoav. "So, young warrior, you have chosen the role of a mute? Say something."

"You know the basic facts. As they say back home, the rest is commentary."

"Well, it so happens that this court is extremely interested in commentary. It often defines the defendant better and more fully than he thinks."

"I do not consider myself to be a defendant," Yoav said firmly. "An unwilling visitor, no doubt. A guest, perhaps. But nothing else."

The Judge did not conceal his irritation. "Why do you think you're so special? Is your own life history so different from that of your companions? By what right do you expect special treatment?"

"Everyone is free."

"Free to do what?"

"To speak or to remain silent."

"If you are so eager to remain silent, it must be because you have things to hide from us. What are they?"

Yoav made a gesture with his hand as if to indicate his disdain for the interrogation. Claudia tried to calm his fears.

"Don't be difficult, Yoav," she said, in a friendly tone. "Do as we do. Tell us anything that comes into your head."

A melancholy light appeared in Yoav's brown eyes. "What do you want? For me to tell the story of my life in front of people I don't know? It's still mine, so far as I'm aware. And so are its secrets. I choose whom I confide in."

Claudia leaned toward him. "Imagine you're telling me, just me alone."

"In other words, the rest of us just don't exist," said Bruce.

Yoav paid no attention to the interruption. Without looking away from Claudia, he said, "I have had parents, friends, unworthy enemies, devoted allies, some less so. And friends I would like to have kept alive. . . . I've been through two wars; I managed to survive, but I've doubtless killed people like you and me with my bombs and my machine guns. In a word, I've encountered death more than once and turned my back on its hideous face. And sometimes, for the enemy, *I* was Death. Is that enough for you?"

Again Razziel felt a twinge of sorrow. Claudia's mischievous smile reminded him of Kali's at the time when they first knew each other and the girl was bent on creating distance between them rather than bringing them closer together. In those days he had sought comfort in telling himself that Kali was no more than a tease, a man-eater. So what was Claudia?

The Judge wrote something in the notebook that lay in front of him; then, without looking up, he began to speak again.

"The only one left is Raz-zi-el. Razziel Friedman."

"Yes?"

"Is that your name?"

"No. It was given to me."

"And your real name, your true name?"

"I don't know."

"You don't know your own name?" said the Judge incredulously. "Didn't you have parents? Didn't they give you a name?"

Razziel chewed his lip. "I don't remember my parents. I don't know anything about my childhood."

"What do you do in life?"

"I wrote it down. I'm the head of a boys' school, a yeshiva in Brooklyn."

"What is a yeshiva?"

"Many things."

"Be more specific."

Razziel had a moment's hesitation: Should he go into detail, talk about how the Zohar was taught to a chosen few? It would be blasphemy.

"A yeshiva is a school where the Talmud is studied," he blurted out, lowering his head.

"The Talmud? And what is that exactly?"

"A body of laws, interpretations, legends, and teachings, whose authors lived in Jerusalem and in Babylon both before and after the destruction of the Temple by the Romans."

"So you're living in the past as well, like the archivist here. What connection can the past possibly have with our age, with your life, with this night?"

"The connection exists. I study. I teach. I help my pupils find within the ancient texts guidance for living in a constantly changing society. I belong to a tradition that holds that everything that concerns the activities of men and their destinies can be found in the Talmud."

"That's too abstract. For a Christian like myself, the Talmud sounds like a collection of dull and disagreeable ideas. Am I wrong?"

Razziel swallowed hard and shrugged. Was this the time to launch into learned exegesis? To recall the respect the Talmud displays toward minority opinions? To relate the lessons in tolerance offered by Shammai and Hillel, who, despite being passionate adversaries, remained friends and allies?

Claudia came to his rescue. "Leave him in peace," she said to the Judge. "Can't you see he's exhausted? We all are."

The Judge eyed her severely. "I am simply doing my duty."

"Perhaps he's not in a mood for games," Claudia replied dryly.

The Judge stared at her with his unnaturally cold and impassive eyes. "And suppose this were not a game?"

Startled, they wondered if they had heard correctly. Was the man really serious? If it was not a game, what was it?

What could it be? Not all games are innocent. Some come dangerously close to cruelty. They can cause suffering. Others lead to remorse.

And death.

Throwing her head back, Claudia was the first to respond. With a forced laugh she said, "You seem absolutely determined to frighten us. But I suppose that's part of the game too. In life, dear Judge, everything comes down to play-acting. Don't you know that? Ever since Sophocles and good old Bill Shakespeare, people have never ceased repeating it: What is life if not a drama? Some plays are long, others short; some comic, some tragic."

"And what about tonight's?" asked the Judge.

"It's for you to reveal it to us. Aren't you the director? Aren't we in your hands?"

"Very true. You are."

"So, tell us: What is this play we are acting in?" Claudia asked.

The Judge shook his head. "Patience, dear lady. For the moment all I can do is to disclose what is at stake in this inquiry." He frowned and went on. "What is at stake is life."

"And therefore death," said Bruce angrily.

"Death as well," replied the Judge.

A heavy, stunned silence fell upon the survivors. There are some words that explode in your brain: at stake, life, death. Once they are uttered, time becomes unstable. It is impossible to go on as if they had not been heard. From now on they have a power of their own, a power no other force can negate.

OUTSIDE, it seemed as if a giant hand were stirring the snow, so as to join the earth with the heavens. The survivors stared intently at each other—Bruce sniggered, George scratched his head, Razziel chewed his lip, Claudia rubbed her hands together, and Yoav clenched his teeth. They all tried to convince themselves that it was all a dream. But no. On this white winter's night what was in itself quite an ordinary incident had taken a fateful turn. Though still obscure, a threat was taking shape.

Razziel looked at his watch. So did George and Yoav. Thirty-two minutes past midnight. The storm still raged, the snow still swirled. Claudia folded her arms across her chest and looked indignant. George tilted his head, sometimes to say yes, sometimes to say no: He found the young woman's resemblance to Pamela more and more striking; both of them had an aura of sensuality he found provocative. Bruce lit a cigarette, removed his red scarf, and put it on again. Razziel thought about his great and strange friend far away.

"My throat's dry," said Claudia. "May I go find some more tea? There's none left in the teapot."

"I'll take care of it myself," replied the Judge. "I'll send someone."

"But I can—"

"You can do all kinds of things," the Judge interrupted, "but you cannot leave this room. You will all remain here. Until the end."

He went out, leaving a sense of dread behind him. What exactly did "until the end" mean from this lover of enigmas? The end of the storm, perhaps? Or simply the night? In a gesture of bravado Bruce hurried after him and tried to open the door. In vain. It only opened from outside.

The room exploded.

Bruce: "He's crazy. This guy's a raving maniac."

Claudia: "Did you say that to raise our morale? If so, you failed."

George: "Maybe he's a dangerous criminal on the run. A murderer."

Bruce: "In other words, we're hostages? That's absurd."

George: "The main thing is not to irritate him. On this point science and history agree. Madmen and criminals should never be crossed."

Bruce: "Let's grovel before him. Kowtow to him. Flatter him and abase ourselves. Let's satisfy all his whims. Is that what you propose?"

Claudia: "George didn't say that. He simply said—"

Bruce: "I don't give a damn what he said. What interests me is to find a way of getting the hell out of here as soon as possible, before this lunatic really attacks us."

Claudia: "Stop shouting! In this place the walls very likely have ears."

Razziel: "Keep calm, my friends. Let us try to keep calm."

Bruce (*to Claudia*): "Stop him!" (*to George*): "Tell him to stop! When he tells us to keep calm it gets on my nerves. If he doesn't shut up I won't be responsible for my actions."

Razziel turned to Yoav, who remained silent, remote, as if the danger did not concern him.

"You're an officer in the Israeli army. You can't be lacking in experience—or imagination. What should we do?"

At once they all fell silent and looked at Yoav, who waited a moment before replying, "Let me think."

"Take your time," said Bruce ironically.

Yoav did not deign to respond. With his hands in his pockets and a furrowed brow, he circled the room, inspecting the walls and the one window, which looked out onto a courtyard. Suddenly he returned to his chair, took a sheet of paper, and dashed off several quick sentences. Then he smiled and invited Claudia to read what he had just written. "It's a love letter. I felt it was the right moment to write it," he said.

Claudia tried not to betray him as she read his message:

> Take care. We are doubtless being observed and overheard. I have a plan. I will tell you what it is. Pass the word discreetly. For the moment, act naturally.

Razziel wondered what the plan could be. If they were dealing with a madman he might drive them all insane too, before . . .

His thought remained incomplete.

To pass the time, each related the circumstances of his or her departure from Kennedy. With the exception of Razziel, they had all taken the fateful flight by chance. Claudia had missed the earlier flight; a monstrous traffic jam had held up her car for an hour just after crossing the Triboro Bridge. Yoav had been due to leave the day before and George on the following day, but last-minute events had caused them to change their plans. Bruce loathed the competing airline, which had the only early-morning flights.

As for Razziel, he had been eager to spend the day alone, delving into readings of Talmudic and medieval texts, getting his bearings in the labyrinth of his memories, as a prelude to meeting his beloved long-lost friend. Why had the latter suggested a meeting in Jerusalem, a city at once so close and so far away? And why at the time of Hanukkah, when there were urgent administrative problems to resolve at his yeshiva? Razziel did not know. But he was convinced that his very special friend knew what he was doing. Paritus never did anything without a reason. There had always been reasons for the times and places of their encounters. In Paris it was to take part in a rabbinical court that had to resolve the case of an *aguna* (a woman abandoned by a husband who refused to grant her a divorce). In London they had taken part in a circumcision ceremony. In Montevideo they eagerly sought the opinion of the celebrated Rav Shushani on an obscure text from the time of the Gaonim. Each time Razziel had been surprised to find himself face-to-face with Paritus: Had his Master orchestrated these events with the sole purpose of meeting him again? Razziel was growing older; his friend was not. Their conversations always unfolded in the same way: Paritus talked about current problems, while Razziel evoked the dark and blurred shadows of the past. "Talk to me about my father," Razziel would say. And his friend and Master would reply, "Of course, of course, I'll tell you about your father, whom you never knew," while continuing to analyze the letter that Hasdai Crescas, the fourteenth-century Judeo-Spanish philosopher, sent to the Jews of Avignon, telling them about the martyrdom of the Jewish community in Barcelona—a pogrom long before the term existed. Two hundred and fifty dead in a single day, among them the philosopher's son, who had just married. Was it so Razziel would stop thinking about *his* father that the old Master directed his attention to the tragedy of the Sephardic Jews in the Middle Ages?

He remembered one of Paritus's sayings: "We derive our grief, as the artist does his inspiration, from the most mysterious point in our being." But Razziel also recalled thinking that one must first ascertain whether grief, like art, is truly within us. Another of the old mystic's sayings: "One day in Jerusalem I met a great kabalist who refused to reveal himself to the world. As I trod on his shadow he uttered a cry, 'You're hurting me!' It was the shadow of a cry, not a cry. Then I understood why he wanted to stay away from other men." Razziel pictured himself in Jerusalem with Paritus, and for a moment he forgot the danger that might be lying ahead for him and his companions.

The Hunchback reappeared, empty-handed, with a sullen look on his face. "The water's been put on to boil. It'll take some time. I can't help that, but don't worry, I'm still at your service."

"I'd prefer a hotel," grumbled Bruce, growing more and more belligerent.

"There are no hotels near here." The Hunchback turned to Claudia. Eager to please her, the best he could do was to parody Shakespeare. "My kingdom for a hotel room. . . ."

Claudia shrugged. Standing beside Yoav, her thoughts were on the man she loved, the only one she had ever loved with such an all-consuming passion.

"What does that mean?" protested Bruce. "You mean there's not a single hotel in this godforsaken place?"

"There is one. But it's a long way off. In fact, even the closest house isn't very near. In weather like this, no car will take you there. And I wouldn't advise you to go on foot."

"What are we going to do?" asked Claudia. "Your judge goes too far. Suppose I threw a first-rate fit of hysterics? Would that do any good? The way things are going—"

The door opened, and it was the Judge who answered her. "No, it would do you no good at all."

Having returned to his seat at the table, he clasped his hands together so as to look more solemn.

"Let us continue. As we shall all be closeted here for some time, it's the best thing we can do."

"And suppose I say I'm not playing?" Yoav said coldly, a veiled threat in his voice.

"That will be duly noted in the report. But that too is part of the game."

"Have I the right to leave, yes or no?"

"To go where?"

"Anywhere."

"On foot?"

"I'm in good shape. I train every morning. I go jogging. I do karate; kung fu as well."

"Take a look at what's happening outside."

"I'm not afraid."

Yoav got up and put on his overcoat. He went to the door and, like Bruce before him, tried to open it without success. At an order from the Judge, the Hunchback pressed an electronic device he kept with him; the door opened, and he left the room with Yoav, observed anxiously but enviously by his companions. Claudia was making ready to follow them when Yoav reappeared alone several seconds later, took off his coat, and let himself sink into a chair.

"I'll wait with the rest of you," he said, assuming an air of resignation.

Claudia offered him her warmest smile in appreciation of this act of solidarity.

"You have done well to return," said the Judge. "But I would not have let you risk your life. You are my guests here. Do not forget that I hold myself responsible for what befalls you. If something is to happen to one of you, it will occur within these walls, under my eyes."

Razziel had the urge to put a simple question to him.

How did he see them: as visitors to be rescued? strangers to be conciliated? guilty people to be condemned? He decided to remain silent, as he had done once before, in a different prison. But on that occasion he had had a point of reference, a friend.

As he busied himself, the Hunchback was reflecting on his own situation. He had lived through more or less similar events before. But why did he feel vaguely uneasy this time?

> *What a strange character, this judge, this master of mine; on some days he inspires horror, on others worship. Ever since I've been in his service, ever since he saved me—that is to say, over the course of twenty years, according to my reckoning, or ten days, according to his—I have sometimes viewed him with gratitude, sometimes with hatred, but never with indifference.*
>
> *I remember the night his last human cargo arrived. That night he surpassed himself in his manipulations. As he's doing now, he played on the emotions of his "guests" as he might on a diabolical musical instrument that only he knew how to play.*
>
> *Little by little, step by step, he bent them to his will by inspiring in them both fear and hope, solidarity and resignation. As tonight, he set himself up as the Judge, taking on the role of God himself, in the way he doled out punishments and rewards.*
>
> *I could have intervened. Perhaps I should have. I didn't dare. I feared his violence. I fear it even more today. He's capable of the worst.* The only transcendence is in evil

is his favorite aphorism. This throws light on his "philosophy," his concept of social ethics—strange words, when applied to him, but he adores big words. He revels in them. As for me, he couldn't care less about whatever I might long for, love, or possess. Whether I dance with joy or cry with shame is all the same to him. Sometimes I tell myself—or, rather, I repeat what he tells me—that I only exist for *him, and I only exist* through *him.*

I know very little about his past, and he knows everything about mine. He knows how that totally banal and stupid accident happened. How my family died. How I attended no funeral. It was the Judge who told me all about it.

In one sense, I'm no more than an extension of him. I am his secretary, bodyguard, messenger. His whipping boy as well? That too. I am also his jester. I could certainly denounce him. But to whom? And what could I say, having lost the right to speak? Should I run away? Where to? By what means? Who would be willing to take me in? Who would want a poor, grimacing cripple who barely knows how to communicate and then with only one man? Besides, don't I owe him my life?

Ah, careful. I must stop and take tea in to our guests. They can't see me, but I see them and I hear them, all thanks to the wonders of modern technology.

Our prisoners are shivering; they're tired. What we ought to be offering them is a good glass of whiskey or brandy. That's what I take when I feel bad or when I'm scared. One evening the Judge forced me to drink. When my mouth stopped swallowing I no longer knew what it was saying. By the fifth or sixth glass I heard myself shouting,

"Here's to you, God, who created man in ecstasy!" Yes, that's what we should be offering our guests: a drink and a bed. I like the cold, myself. I like the transparent silvery flakes as they swirl and sing their beautiful, elusive melodies. I like to watch them as a friend, I like to observe them falling softly, prettily, quietly; they look as if they were coming down toward the earth in an embrace, to caress it and melt into it. I like swallowing them, feeling them in my mouth. For me the true paradise is without doubt made from ice. And, who knows, perhaps from love as well.

What frightens me is fire. It saps my courage. It makes me go back in time—toward agonies that, given half a chance, made me topple into unconsciousness. By no coincidence does fire inhabit hell. But then why does God demand that man's offerings should come to him through fire? God and I are clearly not on the same wavelength. The Judge is. I know perfectly well what he's doing, even if I don't know why he's doing it. Once, at the very beginning, I asked him. He shrugged his shoulders in reply. "Don't try to understand. Do you know why you breathe? Why you close your eyes at night? Life belongs to man, but the meaning of life is beyond him." However, I'm still seeking. He doesn't know, but I'm seeking. Sometimes I wonder if this man isn't the adversary of God. That would explain many things, but I don't know which.

"Are you feeling better?" asked the Judge, his voice neutral but slightly tinged with irony. "No complaints?"

His guests seemed to be relishing their tea. George swallowed his in rapid mouthfuls; Bruce sipped. Yoav was waiting for it to cool. Claudia stroked her mug almost sensually. The Hunchback observed her with a pounding heart. Raz-ziel too was watching her.

"I now have the following point of order to announce to you," said the Judge in official tones.

What new scheme is he going to dream up for tonight? the Hunchback wondered. *I know quite a few of his routines, yet each time he surprises me. I shall end up believing the only thing that interests him is shocking me—me, his servant.*

"We shall now move on to secrets," declared the Judge.

Ah, good, thought the Hunchback. *I might have guessed. The Judge loves secrets. His own life is full of them: his own, mine (which he says he reads in my eyes), those of everyone who passes through his house. He is nourished by them the way his heart is nourished by the blood that runs in his veins.* Reassured, the Hunchback made his way into the adjoining room, where he could observe the prisoners thanks to a cleverly concealed camera.

"Yes, you heard what I said," the Judge continued. "Secrets. I want each of you to recount to me an episode that marked a turning point in your existence. If you are embarrassed to do this in front of the others, write it down. But I warn you: All cheating and all concealment will be severely punished."

"Tell me, Your Honor," said Bruce, with fake hilarity, "may we make things up?"

"Do whatever comes easiest to you," said the Judge, bristling. "Lie, if that's what you feel like doing. But consider the consequences."

Once again, that menacing tone. What were the evidently disastrous consequences he was alluding to?

On his screen the Hunchback could make out the prisoners with perfect clarity. Razziel appeared to be the most uneasy, Claudia seemed pensive, Yoav distracted, George agitated. Bruce, however, who was generally the most irritated and the most irritating of them all, seemed to be enjoying himself.

George was the first to satisfy the Judge's curiosity.

"I remember a beautiful night in summer," he began.

Somewhere in California. A meadow drenched in a sea of fragrance. His girlfriend, Betty, and himself, both students at the same university. She dreamed of becoming a doctor or a nurse, he a physicist. They were in love, their first real love. Warm intimacy. Mutual trust. They swore to be open and true. Shared ecstasy. With their arms around each other between two tides of passion, they had spoken about their lives: his immigrant parents, her illness at the age of ten, her elder sister who had become infatuated with a roving adventurer. . . .

"Yes, it was beautiful, that summer night long ago," George said with a nostalgic smile. "I still remember the stars, the luminous, serene sky."

Then the world collapsed. At the moment of their deepest union, Betty cried out with passion and called him by a name she had never uttered before: "Ronnie . . . I love you. . . . Don't ever leave me, Ronnie."

Bruce chuckled but said nothing. Claudia was waiting for what was to follow. When it did not come she asked, "Did you ever learn who Ronnie was?"

In lieu of a reply, George rubbed his eyes. To erase the memory?

"Maybe it was me," said Bruce.

Nobody laughed.

Claudia spoke about her own first love, her first separation; a turning point. Every meeting was an adventure, every parting was a crossroads. Yet by next morning you've come down to earth, ready to begin again in another bed, another consciousness. Why on earth can't people live alone? Why do our bodies have need of another body to be happy? But these were ephemeral conquests, too episodic, too fleeting, common to too many young girls hungry for love.

She described her first experience of theater. She must have been seventeen, in her senior year. Her class went to see Sophocles' *Antigone* and then a play by Tennessee Williams. For several hours the stage became her magic universe; for several hours language reigned supreme. And she, Claudia, felt liberated at last from time and place, detached from the forces clamoring for her to love or to kill the love within her. She belonged to herself. Outside herself, everything ceased to exist. Her schoolmates, their teachers, her parents—all were thrust aside, forgotten. Hypnotized, she followed the unfolding of the drama, the biting dialogue. She felt the tensions between the characters in her own flesh. It was as if the actors' glances were signals addressed to her alone. It was then she decided to work in the theater.

The next day in class the English teacher, Mrs. Fein, who was a literary critic for a local daily paper, devoted the whole morning to the plays they had seen. She talked about Williams's concept of theater and his attitude to sexuality, about the director's unusual interpretation, and about the quality of the actors' performances. Talking about the latter, she said that their profession was a thankless one, actors give themselves to the public, but their gift is of limited duration. They give the public words written by others, and that is all the public will remember. But what remains of their eloquence and their gestures? Even if some of the spectators are impressed, they are mortal and so is their memory. A person who did not see Sarah Bernhardt playing the part of Phèdre will never be able to appreciate, or even talk about, the breadth and power of her art.

At one point Claudia raised her hand. "Do you have a question?" asked Mrs. Fein. "No," replied Claudia. "I have a statement to make. You have described an injustice to us, and I propose to correct it."

Claudia the magnificent. What hubris! She thought she could right wrongs, rehabilitate the victims of social or natural injustice. Did she not know that only God can do this? But she was young, Claudia, and naïve: an idealist.

"My story is not so grand," said Bruce, "nor so refined."

A young theology student returns home unexpectedly. To look for a lost notebook? To give his beloved mother a kiss? Or, quite simply, to have a square meal, given that for priests earthly nourishment is in more meager supply than words of heavenly wisdom. But never mind. One fine day he returns home. The house is deserted; nothing surprising in this. His father is surely at the office, his mother doubtless visiting a neighbor, his young sister at school. He decides to wait for them. But what's that strange noise coming from the bedroom? Moaning. Mother is ill! he thinks to himself. Alarmed, he rushes upstairs, opens the door, and is rooted to the spot. A man and a woman (his mother's best friend) are on the floor, half naked, making love with a passion that cuts them off entirely from the outside world. His father does not even notice that the door is open. Or that someone, already a hostile stranger, his hand over his mouth, is staring at him, incredulous, ready to howl at the couple, to vomit on love, if indeed *that* was human love.

Bruce now seemed less aggressive. And Claudia's eyes clouded over with sadness for a moment. The Judge only nodded.

"You have done well to confide in us," he said. "We are here to find out the truth before passing sentence."

Bruce recovered his verve and insolence at once. "Sentence? What sentence? What do you take me for? A defenseless vagrant picked up by the police? Or a man on trial? Who gives you the authority? How dare you?"

"I have told you: I am a judge."

"Judge whomever you like, but not me. You very kindly picked us up at the airport: thanks. You offered us hospitality: thanks again. But your kindness does not give you the right to sit in judgment on me. Is that understood?"

"The court takes note of it."

And the Judge conscientiously scribbled a few words on his pad.

Brutally a picture came to Razziel's mind, ripping aside the veils that obscured it. In a faint glow he saw—or saw again—a child on a horse-drawn sleigh, his hair flying in the wind. The child was happy. He was happy because it was snowing. It was snowing in paradise where all is snow.

Yoav was absentmindedly listening to his traveling companions' accounts; they did not move him. Men's petty betrayals had never much interested him, nor had their daily disappointments. Each man was his own executioner and his own victim.

Brooding on the illness that dwelled inside him and sapped his strength, he was trying to imagine not only his own death but how and by whom it would be told.

He was also thinking about Carmela, his childhood sweetheart, beautiful and mischievous, the younger daughter of his neighbors, a couple who were government officials. From their first encounter at the village's kindergarten, she had loved to tease him, to make fun of him and rebuff him in order to attract him. How old was he when he dared to grasp her hand? Five? Eight? They were on the way home from school as usual. The bus stopped beside their two houses. Yoav and Carmela were the only ones to get off. Suddenly Carmela slipped, and Yoav stretched out his hand to catch her. He only let her go after a good while. After that, every day he waited for her to stumble again.

She will be unhappy, thought Yoav. She won't show it, it's not her style to parade her emotions, but she will experience the pangs of mourning, for sure. When he had told her of his illness, without revealing its gravity, she had heard him out to the end with a thoughtful air. Then she had silenced him by kissing him, quite gently at first, then with blazing passion. And as she did each time she wanted to conquer the sadness of his memories of war, she had given herself to him. Together, joined to each other in abandon and plenitude, they would be able to withstand the howling beasts without and all the inner demons within.

Of course, Yoav knew very well that sooner or later he would have to make Carmela understand that love, too, is powerless against this deadly disease. She had the right to know, but Yoav had never found it easy to translate his feelings—or even his thoughts—into words. Instead of explaining himself he would retreat into silence. Was it because the soldier in him, accustomed to giving orders, confined himself to brief remarks? He suffered from a shyness that sometimes made him seem hostile. He trusted actions more than words. A raised eyebrow or a shrug of the shoulders is often more eloquent than an elaborate statement. And yet gestures can also be inadequate, even ludicrous, when called upon to express things as simple as illness and death. But Carmela had understood. She could often read the thoughts of the man she loved. "Don't say anything, not a word; leave it to me." How often had she whispered these words to him, like a litany, to calm his anxiety, either before he went off on a mission or on his return? Thus she would always contrive to restore his peace of mind, except for one occasion. . . .

A memory. It is dark. The silence is oppressive. A moonless night, strewn with obstacles and deadly traps. Seven men with lowered heads are advancing in silence into enemy territory. All their senses on the alert, they walk slowly, as if over a minefield. The darkness must not be disturbed. The grass must not be stopped from growing, the foliage from resting. Death has a thousand eyes, which attract life in order to extinguish it. To elude their power you must conceal and clothe in death everything that resembles a living body. Down below, the Arab village appears asleep. It is from there that their prey will emerge: two terrorists, covered in explosives and disguised as peasants on the way to Jerusalem to spill Jewish blood. No guard posted around the village. The guys from military intelligence have done their job well; this spot is ideal for a lookout.

At a sign from Yoav, his second in command, Shmulik, climbs a tree. With his infrared field glasses he scans the horizon. The next moment he is back on the ground. "Nothing," he whispers. "Nothing at all." Yoav touches his shoulder. "It's early yet. Their rendezvous with the agent is scheduled for one hour before sunrise. You've got time to go back up again. Just keep an eye on things." "And if it goes wrong?" asks Shmulik. "You'll know what to do," says Yoav. Shmulik nods; if there's any snag he will be in a good position to use his machine gun.

They have no need to spell things out to understand one another, Yoav and Shmulik. They have been together since the start of their military service. They are more than brothers in arms. They are bound to one another, inseparable. No wonder that Carmela, without ever admitting it, sometimes feels a little jealous.

In a low voice, Yoav briefs his men on their stations and gives them precise instructions: radio silence, no smoking, no fire until the Arab terrorists will have left their guide.

They all settle down into the night, following a tried and

tested strategy, seeking to make themselves invisible in the darkness. Members of an elite unit, they have taken part in more than one operation of this kind. Their team spirit, their almost organic cohesion and quick collective reflexes insure their unequaled place in Israel's heroic legend. Logically, the ambush should proceed without a hitch. Besides, as Shmulik says, "I wonder why we're taking so many precautions. Quite apart from the element of surprise, we're seven against two: What risk is there?"

But that night events took a different turn. They had fallen into a trap. Dug in well in advance, the enemy was waiting for them. And when, shortly before dawn, the two terrorists appeared, accompanied by a third Arab, Yoav and his unit had no time to rally; shells were falling on all sides and machine guns were crackling, spitting deafening and hateful fire in their direction. "Yoav!" cried Shmulik. "What the . . . ? Yoa-a-av. . . ."

Two helicopters came to the rescue of what was left of the unit. The next day Yoav took part in his friend's military funeral. And for weeks thereafter he kept seeing Shmulik in his dreams, doubled up in pain, dying with his name on his lips. Carmela stayed by his side, she kept murmuring, "Let it all come out. . . . I'm here, look at me. . . ."

He looked at her, and what he saw was Shmulik, covered in blood, his right arm torn off, close beside his knee, a grotesque and useless object. Always the same image: A gentle wind gathered up a few clouds, then began blowing them into the distance, dragging Shmulik along behind them, like a shroud. An odd notion haunted Yoav's mind: If I die who will tell Lidia the truth about Shmulik's death, and the truth about Shmulik the man?

His friend's death continued to obsess him. Strangely, he did not remember the noise of the bullets that had filled the valley that night. It was as if Shmulik had died in total cosmic silence. He remembered having murmured, "Shmulik's dead." Then, in a louder voice, "Shmulik is dead!" In the end he imagined he had shouted, *"Listen, everyone, my friend Shmulik is dead!"* as if he needed to convince himself. He did not completely believe it. Something in him refused to accept that a man like Shmulik, who had so often looked death in the eye, could be snuffed out like a candle in the wind. Deep inside him he still saw Shmulik not as dead but as having gone far away, to a place where true reunions happen, true bonds, eternal ones, are forged.

In his hand, Yoav holds the letter that was found in Shmulik's pocket: "To be given to Captain Yoav or his wife, Carmela, if something happens to me." It contained his truth. It had to do with Lidia.

The only and spoiled daughter of well-off Hungarian parents, Lidia had laid claim to her future husband in a seaside café in Tel Aviv. Young people, all from "nice" families, used to the good life and partying, often gathered there to discuss their pressing affairs of the heart, half seriously and half in jest. Some of them were just back from some kind of ashram in India; others were describing their adventures in Europe.

Shmulik happened to be there one evening with Yoav, both of them in uniform. Sitting in a corner of the terrace, they were discussing a political play they had just seen at the National Theater. Suddenly a tall blond girl appeared before them. Her hands on her hips, sure of herself and of the effect she was having on the men, she stationed herself in front of Yoav.

"My name's Lidia. And you? What's your name?"

"Why do you want to know?"

"I find you appealing."

"Thank you, I'm flattered. But—"

"But what?"

"I'm not free—"

"Free to do what?" She dared him. "To love me? Not even for an evening? An hour? Men don't usually turn me down."

Yoav felt himself blushing; she was beautiful and attractive, this blond girl. Everything about her suggested voluptuousness.

"I'm sorry," he said, repressing a sigh. "I don't wish to offend you, but—"

"But what?" She stamped her foot. "You're married? And she keeps you on a leash like a dog, is that it?"

"No, that's not it. I'm engaged. I love my fiancée, and I love her freely. *Because* I love her I am free."

The girl stared at him angrily, contemptuously, and turned to Shmulik.

"I like the look of you too. Don't tell me that, unfortunately, you too are stupid."

"No," replied Shmulik, laughing. "No girl has succeeded in catching me yet."

"None? That's fine. Say goodbye to your bachelor life. Hey, you haven't told me your name. And as for you, Mr. Freedom, you'll pay for this, I promise you."

Shmulik and Lidia became inseparable. Finally they married. They became neighbors of Yoav and Carmela. Their houses in the village of Herzliya became havens of happiness, until the fateful day when Lidia found a way of exacting her revenge.

It was a Saturday. Yoav walked over to see Shmulik, who was not at home.

"He'll be back any minute now," Lidia told him. "Come and wait for him in the living room."

He sat down in his usual spot on the sofa, near the telephone, with his back to the window. Lidia brought him a glass of orange juice and settled on his left. They talked of vacations, concerts, tensions on the Lebanese border, the election campaign. Then, suddenly, Lidia grew somber.

"Do you think Shmulik's happy?"

"Yes, I think so. Thanks to you, he's a happy man."

She fell silent, listless, and finally burst out, "Well, I'm not, I'm not happy!"

Taken by surprise, all Yoav could do was to stammer. "Why . . . why do you say that?"

"Because I can't take it anymore. You hear me? I can't take it anymore. I can't keep on bottling it all up inside me: my desires, my fears, the real me. I don't love him, I don't love myself, in fact, I'm sick of myself. I want love, my body wants love. I've had enough, you hear me? I've had enough of living like this."

Yoav had never seen her like this: hysterical, as if possessed by a dybbuk. She was out of breath, her face contorted. To calm her he took her hand but let go of it at once. He felt embarrassed and, vaguely, at risk. He got up and made for the door, murmuring childish excuses and words of appeasement, whereupon, with one furious motion, she barred his way.

"Oh, no. Don't think you can turn your back on me this time!" she screamed. "You rejected me once. You humiliated me. Don't you think once is enough? Once is enough, I tell you!"

"I don't know what you're talking about," said Yoav. "You must have had too much to drink. Go lie down; take a nap; you'll feel better. . . ."

He tried to break free but she resisted, flinging her arms around his neck. Yoav was surprised by her strength, as she drew him to her. A moment later he felt her lips on his. And then, as in a vaudeville routine, at this precise moment Shmulik appeared. Thunderstruck, he stepped outside, as if he did not wish to appear indiscreet. Overcome with fright and perhaps with remorse, Lidia ran after him, crying out, "You don't understand. . . . I can explain everything!" They disappeared into the garden and Yoav went home stunned, as if in mourning.

"What's happened? Have you had an accident?" Carmela asked him. "I'm afraid I may just have lost my best friend," he replied.

Some hours later, after dinner, Shmulik came to see him. Carmela was clearing the table. She withdrew to let them talk. Shmulik took a chair and sat down facing his friend, then changed his mind.

"Lidia has told me everything," he said stonily.

Yoav waited to hear what followed.

"She says you're in love with her, madly in love with her, and always have been."

Yoav listened aghast.

"She also said it wasn't the first time you'd tried to kiss her."

Yoav remained silent. As he stared into space in front of him, his head began to feel as if it were caught in a vise of steel. What should he say, what should he do? Condemn his friend's wife at the risk of breaking up their marriage? Take it all upon himself and lose the friendship of a man he respected and whose respect mattered to him as much as his own true love for Carmela? He was at sea, his head seething with words and images. He, who always knew what to do and what orders to give his men in the most unexpected situations, now felt helpless, barren of any idea or initiative. He knew only one thing: He needed a miracle.

And the miracle took place. Thanks to Carmela, who had heard and understood everything.

"Shmulik," she said, returning to the dining room, "there's something I want you to know: Lidia loves you. She adores you. She has never loved anyone but you."

The two men turned to stare at her at the same moment. "Don't look so stricken," she went on. "The situation has always been crystal clear to me, and I'm not going to change my mind today. Yoav is your best friend, so he can hardly help feeling fond of Lidia, but it's the fondness of a friend, not of a lover, and this is what Lidia must have misinterpreted. My love for Yoav is not affected. Nor should your friendship for him be. Yoav has done nothing wrong, nothing irreparable, and neither has Lidia, believe me. What happened just now never happened before. And will never happen again. I give you my word."

She talked for a long time, determined at all costs to convince Shmulik of the truth of her explanations. Finally she sent him home. "Your wife is waiting for you. Go and reassure her. She needs you."

Shmulik, who had been watching her, almost in a trance, was transfigured and had to make an effort to come back to reality. He went to Carmela and kissed her on the cheek.

"You are simply wonderful," he told her. "You are extraordinary. Yoav is very fortunate to have you as his ally." And he added with a smile, "What amazes me is that I haven't fallen in love with you myself."

Once the door had closed behind him, Yoav was about to say something but Carmela stopped him.

"I know. I know what you're going to say to me: I'm mad. Of course I'm mad: madly in love with you. Why do you think I became involved in this silly business? Not just to save their marriage but, above all, to save your friendship. I thought my explanation would be less painful for him."

Yoav looked at her hard. "But you do know the truth, don't you?"

"Of course I know."

"It was Lidia who—"

"Please don't say another word, my love. I know you. You have never left me, not even in your dreams."

Yoav taunted her: "Aren't you being a bit too sure of yourself? Sure that I have never lied to you?"

She took his head in her hands. "Well, that would mean that our truth was a lie, and that would be stupid, ridiculous, and completely crazy."

They began laughing like happy children.

The next day Lidia brought them a bottle of great vintage wine to thank Carmela for her "understanding."

"Thanks to you, we're drunk with our love."

The two men never again referred to the incident that

could have put an end to their friendship, but in his posthumous letter Shmulik revealed to his friend that he had not been deceived.

> Carmela is an angel of kindness, affection, and understanding, but I know the truth for I know Lidia. She would be vexed with me for telling you, but in the end she confessed everything to me. This only made your own action all the more meaningful. You were ready to sacrifice yourself and our friendship in order to protect my illusory happiness. Thank you, my friend.

At the bottom of the page there was a postscript.

> You know how much I have loved dreaming and fighting by your side but don't be in a hurry to join me. Take your time.

Confronting Lidia, Yoav could not bring himself to speak. He would have liked to talk about her husband's heroism, tell her that he shared her grief, talk to her about the real Shmulik, but, as ever, he could not find the words. Face-to-face with the young woman, he agonized over what words to use. There was no need. Lidia took one look at him, and naked, brutal grief covered her face like a mask. She sank into a chair and remained there motionless for hours, feeling the sap draining from her world.

. . .

Bent over his files, the Judge addressed Razziel without looking at him. "It's your turn."

A turning point? Which one? An episode, an event? From what period? His days in prison? Earlier? But his earlier life was veiled in darkness.

"What do you expect of me? What do you want me to say to you?"

"Speak."

"What about?"

"Whatever you wish."

"About whom?"

"Not just anyone. Tell us about someone who has mattered in your life."

"Very well," said Razziel. "His name is Paritus."

"What was he to you?"

"A support. A voice in the shadows. A reflection of the secret universe. A Master. A storyteller. A kind of well digger, one who knows how to detect the springs that water the soul."

Razziel recalled a story that Paritus had recounted to him.

"In the street, the celebrated Maharal of Prague meets his noble friend the Emperor Rudolph, who asks him where he's going. 'I do not know, sire,' replies the Jewish sage. 'Come now, are you making fun of me? You have left your house to go somewhere, and you really don't know where you're bound for?' 'No, Your Majesty, I do not know.' Incensed, the king has him arrested and put in prison for high treason. But when he comes before the judge, here's how the Maharal justifies his remarks: 'What did I say to His Majesty that was not true? I told him I did not know where I was going. Was I not right? When I left my house I thought I was going to the synagogue—and yet here I am in prison.' "

Razziel told this story not to obey the Judge but to please Claudia, who reminded him distantly of Kali. At this moment of uncertainty, he had only one thought, one wish: He longed to be able to begin all over again with Kali, to see her again. Perhaps to follow her into death.

"I like listening to you," Kali used to say to him, taking his hand.

"But I haven't said anything."

"I like listening to you even when you aren't saying anything."

They were happy. They needed so little to forget all that threatened their happiness. To take walks along the Hudson River. To share a raspberry ice. To watch the children playing in the park. To listen to a record. To guess the contents of a book before opening it. What would his life have been without this woman who was like no other?

"We love one another and yet we're so different," Kali remarked to him one day, pressing him to her heart. "To really fall in love, must one avoid people who resemble one?"

"We love one another, isn't that enough?"

"It's not enough. We're similar but not identical."

"How are we different?"

"In everything, for heaven's sake!"

"You're right," he said, mocking her, "I'm a man and you're a woman."

"No, no, I'm not talking about that. I'm talking about—"

"What *are* you talking about?"

In fact she was right. She came from a large wealthy family. Her father, a pious Jew much devoted to the Hasidic world, had been a diamond merchant in Antwerp and now lived in a fine apartment in Brooklyn. She was a lawyer in a Manhattan law firm. Razziel, on the other hand, barely knew who he was.

He often wondered how she could love him, this unattractive traveler without luggage, a wanderer who could offer her nothing.

"I like to surprise you," she told him.

In truth, nothing really surprised him, though he would marvel at the falling of a leaf in the wind, a nocturnal noise, a stranger's smile; what he lacked was a childhood, the period that prepares a man for growing up, for storing away memories in his mind, emotions in his heart. And yet, deep within, he responded to all that happened to him, good or bad, as if he had already lived through it in the past. And this was a mystery that only Paritus could resolve.

When Razziel abandoned his nostalgic meditation, Kali vanished into the shadows. In neutral tones and maintaining his severe and taciturn air, the Judge had just made a suggestion that caused him to sit up with a start.

"In the game we are playing tonight, one essential element is lacking: Death. Let us invite Death to join us, if only to take the game, let us say, more seriously."

Looking at no one in particular, he continued. "I put this problem to you: Picture, if you will, that one of my people, a seer, has read in the stars that one of the individuals taking part in this little gathering here is to die tomorrow. In consternation he has asked his Master to explain this vision to him. The latter has uttered the appropriate prayers, and the voice of heaven has replied to him, 'Since humanity has entered into a period of moral decline, God demands a human sacrifice in order to hold back from punishing *all* humanity.' The problem is: Who is to be the scapegoat? And who will assume the role of executioner?"

He fell silent, ran his hand over his brow, and continued. "I leave you to consider."

After a stunned silence Bruce burst out laughing, but his laughter sounded hollow. George stared open-mouthed at a point in space.

"Now listen to me, Judge," Bruce said. "You can tell your man of visions to go to the devil, and if the devil won't have him, tell him to marry the old village witch. Let him get it out of his system and leave us in peace."

Looking incredulous, Claudia shook her head. "First you interrogate us. Now you give us your hallucinations. What are you getting at? I like theater, I like games, but not sick games. We're not in a circus as far as I know. Are we by any chance in a lunatic asylum? Are you offering us a psychodrama? Generally, psychodrama is used for therapy. Whom are you trying to cure?"

The Judge listened impassively.

"There's no sick person here to be cured," Claudia went on. "We're all in perfectly good health, thank God. So what's the idea? What's the point of this performance? At least have the decency to tell us."

The Judge remained silent.

Claudia resumed. "We're dying of hunger and exhaustion, and all you're interested in doing is playing childish games."

"And why not?" replied the Judge, suddenly serene. "Whether he is in mortal danger or is simply at play, man always goes back to his childhood. And if this is only a game, it's an innocent one. Why not say you will take part in it, just to please me?"

An irrefutable argument: How could they refuse their savior a brief hour of enjoyment? Surely as his guests they owed him that.

"All right," said Claudia grudgingly. "Let's get on with it."

"Thank you. So someone here is going to die tomorrow. It could be any one of you. To begin with, I advise you all to prepare yourselves. No doubt you have letters to write, wills to draw up, farewells to make. . . . I repeat: Do not forget that for one of you this night could be your last."

A stormy debate ensued: How far should this puerile game be taken?

"What's this madman going to dream up next?" yelled Bruce. "He's out of his mind, for God's sake! What he needs is a psychiatrist! And a straitjacket!"

"Calm down," said George, in a weary voice. "What's the good of losing your temper? It's only a game. Let's go along with it."

Razziel rubbed his eyes. His head was spinning, his brain

was exploding, and his pen slid across the paper without leaving a mark. He took refuge in thoughts of Kali: "All the things I haven't told you. . . ." They should have had children, but God had decided otherwise. Then he thought of his pupils: What would become of them? Of Meir, the *Ilui*, the genius of the group: a young man who had come from far, from the world of temptation and sin, and had succeeded in climbing rapidly up the ladder of knowledge. Would he be his successor? Does Paritus know the answer? And, even if he does, will we ever meet again?

The Judge consulted his watch, made a vague gesture, picked up his papers, and went out. He instructed the Hunchback, who was waiting for him in the corridor, not to leave his observation post.

Outside, the snowflakes were dancing lightly, like drunken images in the incandescent minds of the prisoners.

The document, what can I do about the document? pondered George, with a pang of anguish. If something happens to me there's a risk of its falling into the wrong hands, and that would be a disaster. What can be done? Absentmindedly, he took part in the others' conversation. Trying to conceal his anxiety, he focused on his recent discovery in the National Archives, a serious and sensational discovery that implicated an important political personality in Europe. He was due to discuss this in Israel with a historian, a colleague whom he trusted, a man who had access to Mossad.

Suddenly, something made him pay attention. Once again Razziel had uttered a strange name that opened a forgotten door in his memory. He sat up straight and asked, "Paritus? Did you say Paritus?"

"Yes," replied Razziel, in astonishment. "Does that name mean anything to you? You haven't come across him by any chance?"

"Sure, I've come across him. Many times."

Razziel could not control his excitement. "When? How? In what circumstances? Where did you meet him?"

"At the National Library, of course," George replied with a laugh.

"He came there?"

"He's there now."

Razziel looked so dumbfounded that George had a moment of doubt. "Are we talking about the same person?" Then he explained. He had read and studied the writings of Paritus. The first of these dealt with "The Mystery of Absence" in medieval Jewish theology. The second was a mystical poem evoking God's nostalgia for the time before time that had preceded the Creation. The third was a meditation on the Apocalypse. Intrigued by the author, George had sought to know more about him. It seemed he had lived in Safed in the fifteenth century, visited Spain, traveled through the Rhineland, and ended his life somewhere in eastern Poland.

Fascinated, his lips half open as if to catch the words as they flew past, Razziel uttered little cries, swiftly suppressed, as he listened to the archivist. "Are you certain? Tell me, are you really certain of this?"

"Certain? Yes, I'm certain the author of these texts was called Paritus. He's the 'one-eyed Paritus' referred to by a contemporary of Spinoza. He wrote his works as he traveled through distant lands—" He broke off and lowered his voice, "I've even managed to get hold of a manuscript by this grievously little-known writer. It's very short, only twenty pages, but its value is inestimable. The subject? You'd never guess: immortality."

The others chattered away, but Razziel and George were in a world of their own. Brought together by the name, if not the person, of Paritus, nothing could separate them now.

"You must come and visit me one day," said George. "I'll show you his work. But what am I saying? You must know it, because I think I heard you say you had come across him . . . but is it the same man? Is it possible? The Paritus I know lived five centuries ago."

Razziel, lost in thought, did not reply immediately. He broke his silence by asking another equally disturbing question: "What if Paritus were immortal?"

George smiled. "Isn't that true of all mystics? I mean, doesn't their quest make them immortal?"

In his mind Razziel continued this line of inquiry with yet another question: Can't one say the same thing of the profane and of criminals, the enemies of mankind and God? Do they not all outlive their victims? When I see Paritus again, he said to himself, I must ask his opinion.

I WAS BORN at the age of eighteen," Razziel confided to George Kirsten. "I don't say that as a provocation but because it's the truth. The truth has nothing to do with numbers.

"In point of fact, I may have been seventeen. Or twenty. I no longer know. I'm no longer sure of anything having to do with my childhood and adolescence. When I think about my early years I'm lost in a fog. But I know I was born long after my actual birth. A remarkable man told me this. He's the only person in the world who can help me. In fact, he already helped me in the past, and now I'm waiting to meet him and he's waiting for me. He will return into my life. He has promised me. It is either his surname or his given name, I never knew which, that I bear within me and that sustains me.

"He is all I can remember. As for the rest, I've forgotten everything except the place: a prison cell. And the time: dawn. Or dusk. What difference does it make? It's the same struggle: for or against the light. For it to break through or to fade. At a certain moment, a human voice made its way into me and caused me to be born into the world. Why a human voice? Are some voices not human? Certainly there is the voice of God, but it is made of fire and silence. There is the voice of the nocturnal beast, harrying its prey before striking it down, but that voice is a harbinger of death. There is the voice of the tree, calling to the wind, and that of the rocks. And that of the madman plowing furrows in time. No, the voice I heard was a human one. At first it caused me pain; I felt an unfamiliar tugging at my insides. Should I shout? Yell? I didn't yet know how.

"When did the voice become as pleasant and soothing as balm? Later, much later. It made me understand that I was no longer alone. There was someone there in my cell, someone who breathed as I did and who, like me, was embedded in the darkness. I didn't know who it was, but I knew it was a human being. I knew this not from having been told by someone but from having understood it for myself. I knew it, just as I know I should have a face, a voice, and a place in the sun, just as I know that in my neighbor's eyes I am certainly a stranger, perhaps an intruder.

"In fact, it took me some time, first to locate him and then to identify him. He had a beard. Instinctively I put my hand to my chin, convinced that, like his, it was covered in hair. Disappointed, I lowered it. At once I felt myself reeling. I recognized my state of inferiority. A beard—a real one—apparently has to be earned. Or won in battle. To dispel my malaise I closed my eyes. In the dark everything should feel better. Like before, prior to my birth. But nothing now was like before. The darkness into which I plunged was no longer the same. It no longer protected me; I was no longer alone.

"The man observing me, shrouded in shadow and silence, was someone I had never met. Would he be a brother to me? My enemy perhaps? Where did he come from? How had he managed to arrive in this cell before I did? Should I ask him? Certainly not. Despite my lack of experience of life, I knew that the more you ask certain questions, the more dangerous they become. What if this other one, facing me, were simply my double, my real me? On no account should I make a fool of myself. Fortunately, he spoke first. He cleared his throat several times and asked, 'Do you recall?'

"I didn't understand the meaning of his question. Since I was no longer—or not yet—in possession of a past, I had no idea how I could have remembered it. Surprised by my silence, he repeated his question.

" 'So? Tell me if you recall.'

"I was suddenly struck by the soothing quality of his voice. I would have liked it to be mine. To verify whether this was so, I thought it best to open my mouth.

" 'No, yes,' I said, very quickly.

" 'Yes or no?'

" 'Both,' I replied, speaking faster and faster. 'I start with no and end with yes. But the two are the same.'

"He began nodding his head, as if overcome by great joy or terrible sadness. 'If it's yes, who and what do you recall?'

" 'Someone who only knows how to say no.'

"Why did I utter these words? There was an obscure urge in me that made me say no, always no. No, no, a thousand times no. No to what and to whom? Until when? I had no idea.

"The stranger was silent for a while. His whole body was swaying, as if he were shaken by a fever. A shiver ran through me: Perhaps he was sick; was he going to die before my eyes and leave me alone here? Was he going to die in my place or take me with him? I was relieved when he began to speak again.

" 'Do you remember who I am?'

"I didn't remember.

" 'Do you remember who you are?'

"I didn't remember.

"He sighed deeply. 'Do you really recall nothing?'

" 'Nothing.' Was he disappointed? It was clear he was in distress. My inability to satisfy his curiosity distressed him. How could I explain to him that it was not my fault? That a being who has only just been born has no memories? 'Give me time to breathe,' I told him."

I have memories. But they only concern things that happened later. I am willing to talk about them. Isn't that what the Judge demands, for me to tear away the veil covering everything that is hidden or nebulous in what he calls my past? He claims he wants to understand. To understand in order to judge better. Will he accuse me, convict me, repudiate me, before eliminating me? Suppose I were to plead guilty? Should I invite punishment as the ultimate way out? No. My friend will come to my aid. Paritus will liberate me, I'm sure of it. He will come; he promised me. I've learned a lot from him. I've learned that man's special capacity is for waiting, his ability to reconcile his own time with that of God.

You've guessed it. My great friend, the friend of my lost youth, is my former cellmate. One day he said to me, "Living outside the law is neither good for the mind nor good for the heart, but does not living in itself make one guilty—I mean, guilty of living?" I had an impulse to reply to him, But if *all* living people are guilty, can't we deduce from this that no one is? I said nothing. I said nothing because I was struck by the strange reality that, even if I was right, no one has the words to express it.

I think about my friend; I know he's waiting for me where we agreed to meet, in Jerusalem, close by the Wall. So is he far away? I know that, even when we first met, he was distant from me. Even when, feeling my way, I tried to come closer to the corner where he was crouching, the distance between us did not diminish. When he uttered a question here, a remark there, his voice became dense; it blinded me. I was too small, almost a newborn babe; I could hardly see him; I saw him without knowing who it was I saw or even that I could see. This lasted for a time that today seems both inexplicably short and infinitely long. On his lips, words became corporeal and were transmuted into objects, but these objects had a life of their own that made them pulsate, leap in the air, and fall to earth, exhausted. It was only later that I understood. In friendship the ego is not dissolved in the other; on the contrary, it blossoms. Unlike love, friendship does not declare that one plus one makes one; rather, that one plus one makes two. Each of the two is enriched by and for the other. "In some religions," my companion would tell me, "man must die in order to be reborn. I am opposed to this. I am against death, and against those who bring death, and against those who love death. One must never use death as a means—not even in the name of life."

Sometimes he spoke little. He listened. He spoke only to oblige me to reply—so he could continue to listen.

"What is your name?"

"I don't know."

It was the truth; I did not know that men give names to one another.

"Don't you have a name?"

"What is a name?"

"It's the first gift a child receives from its parents."

"I have never received a gift. I never had any parents. Look: I've just been born and there's no one to give me any warmth."

"I'm here."

"You're there, but I can't feel you. I don't remember you. I don't remember anyone."

"Try to remember. Make an effort. Think about the word *before.* It's an important word."

Very well. With eyes closed I seized upon the word and began to cradle it gently, then to feel it, then to grip it with all my strength. *Before*—before what? Before whom? I was looking for a face, just one, no matter whose, a human face, not a mask. I ended up feeling a sharp pain in my head, the first in my life. Since then it has never left me.

While I was rummaging within myself, he kept up a commentary. He strove to convince me that every man is born of parents; that every man is attached to a childhood; that we all have a memory, which may sometimes resemble a bedroom, sometimes a castle in flames. Both can be unlocked; all you need to do is find the key. He repeated these last words several times, so much so that I cried out, "Fine, fine, the key. All I need to do is find it. But where is it, this key?"

Astonished by the vehemence of my question, he got up. Now, even in the half-light, I could see him better. He was tall; his head touched the ceiling. I could see his face as well; it was etched with a nameless grief. What was the light that glowed in his somber eyes? And why did he keep his lips shut even when he was speaking? I studied him for a moment and thought, *This is a man.*

Suddenly he leaned toward me and spoke to me slowly, separating each syllable. "The key that you seek, that we will seek together, is hidden within yourself." Then, after taking a long breath: "No. The key you seek is not only within you; it *is* you."

Leaning back against the wall, he let himself slide down to resume his seat on the ground.

We talked all night—or was it day? When had I seen the sun rise or set? Our cell was located in a basement. A dusty lightbulb hanging from the ceiling gave off a feeble light. I later learned that, in order to disorient the prisoners, the jailers deprived them of all points of reference. "Meals" were always passed to us through the spyhole by an invisible prisoner—I never saw more than an arm—and always at different times.

My cellmate explained the oddness of my condition to me this way: My inquisitors had succeeded in stealing my memory. That's it. They had simply filched it and carried it off to another prison within this prison. To what end? To this question my cellmate, though he was very well-informed, had no answer. "One day you'll know," he said.

How many days and weeks had I been there, confined within those leprous walls? "For seven times seven nights," replied my cellmate, who was becoming my guide and companion. The official interrogations had long since come to an end. Now it was he who asked the questions. "It may well be that they have inadvertently left behind a fragment of an episode, a snatch of a phrase that could give us a clue." He made vague mention of a plump policeman who hissed like a snake when he was out of breath: Did I remember him? A sadistic guard who played with a razor, as if preparing to slash the flesh of the accused? A silent nurse with a syringe she always carried; the first torture by means of prolonged insomnia—no, no, I had no memory of those. I remembered nothing. As soon as I looked into the past I felt I was hovering over a dark, opaque ocean. And a familiar anxiety arose within me, stopping my breath: I was afraid I was slipping, falling, drowning in myself. Refusing to be discouraged, my protector threw both simple and complicated words at me, sharp and blunt words, pausing after each of them, as if in permanent expectation of a miracle that did not, in fact, occur, that was not going to occur. The start of a dream, a vague image? Nothing, always nothing. Finally, exhausted, sadness overcame him and he remained silent for a long time before admitting defeat.

"Since you cannot remember who you are, I shall tell you who I am and, more precisely, who I shall be for you."

He leaned toward me and clasped my shoulder with his two hands.

"My name is Paritus. I repeat: Pa-ri-tus. You say it now: Pa-ri-tus."

I took a breath and said, "Pa-ri-tus."

"Good. Now, my given name: Razziel. I repeat: Razziel. You say it now: Raz-zi-el."

I took a breath and said, "Raz-zi-el."

"Very good. Paritus is only a nickname. My real name, Razziel, was given me by my parents. When we part you will keep it for yourself. You will keep it until the day you find your own name again. Agreed?"

"Yes, agreed. But who are you?"

"A messenger."

"Where do you come from?"

"I was born in the mountains far away."

"Are you alone?"

"My parents were killed."

"Brothers?"

"Massacred."

"Sisters?"

"Assassinated."

"And you are their messenger?"

"Yes, but they are also mine."

"And I? Who am I?"

"One day you will know."

"When?"

"When you meet a mad prophet."

"And you, who are you?"

"You will know one day."

"When?"

"When you are free. Free as I shall be. Free as artists are, artists who see farther than prophets."

This exchange exhausted me. I found it hard to breathe. I asked to rest a moment. I closed my eyes and called upon sleep, which only came in fits and starts. Razziel Paritus slept as well, but he seemed to be keeping his eyes open. What could he see when there was nothing to see?

That night, or that day—how can I tell which?—he told me of my arrival in the cell: I had a quite deathly appearance; my body and my gaze were drained of life.

"There were several of us who saw you," my friend said. "An impatient one, who was angry because the letter he was waiting for had got lost in the mail, and a silent one, who understood everything but only responded with his eyes. You were different. You were not only outside language but also outside the passage of time. Time washed over you, maybe even flowed through you, without leaving a trace. The silent one stared at you intently; you paid no attention. The impatient one shook you; you let him do it. I myself dreamed up a thousand devices for rousing you from your torpor. To no avail. Were you somewhere else? You were nowhere. I understood that it was better to abandon the attempt: In prison you always pay a price for vain efforts. A few days later we were separated from the silent one and the impatient one; either they were put in another cell or they were taken to the cellar to be shot in the back of the neck. I was left alone with you—which is to say, more alone than without you.

"In the beginning you fascinated me; I wondered who you were and what they could have forced you to endure to reduce you to the state of a wreck whose only human attribute was the misery overwhelming him. I began asking you questions again. I thought that if I continued to question you I would be able to break through the carapace that surrounded you. Did you hear me? You appeared to be deaf and dumb and blind. I scratched a polished metal surface but couldn't get a hold on you. How to explain, how to conquer your lethargy? You ate almost nothing; you hardly drank; your face remained immobile, impenetrable. I grew irritated. I insulted you; I tweaked your ears. You were somewhere else, in a prison more impregnable than our own.

"Suddenly, I became alarmed. You made me doubt myself. My confidence in the future was sapped. Your indifference frightened me. You see, for me, indifference is the sign of sickness, a sickness of the soul more contagious than any other. I knew contact with it would lead me to become its accomplice or its victim. I would be dead before I died. How could I immunize myself against its poison? I knew only one remedy to counteract the effects of dementia on another person: to root it out. It's as simple as that. So as not to become mad like you, a corpse like you, I needed to eliminate *your* madness. And since I quickly understood that your malady took the form of forgetfulness, I decided that the way to heal your impaired if not totally emptied memory was to introduce elements of my own into it.

"To set an example for you, I danced, I sang, I clapped my hands, I scratched myself with my dirty nails, I made faces, I hurled oaths, I recited prayers. I needed to show you that to be a man is also to do all that. I talked to you about God and about my passion for human suffering: Desire is both strength and fire. Then I conveyed to you my rage against God and especially against those who claim to be speaking, yelling, and acting brutally in his name—as if God had a precise name, as if this name were not unutterable. I told you sad stories from my childhood, letting my tears flow. Then, to make you laugh, I told you happy stories. Finally, I lost my temper. And all the time you listened, like a good boy, without moving a muscle, without raising an eyebrow; you were as unresponsive to all my sallies as a stone statue.

"In the end, I would seize you violently and hit your chest so hard it left us both breathless. 'Wake up, for God's sake!' I would yell. 'It's our only chance! One of us is going to win in the end! And if it's not me we're both lost!' Vain efforts, pointless tears. You occupied a fortress I was barred from entering.

"And then one day, or one night—how can one tell one type of twilight from another?—you looked at me and I understood that either you or I or both of us were worthy of miracles. You were looking at me in the same way as before, but more intently. You were drinking in my gaze; you were hearing my voice; you were absorbing my words. I wanted to laugh or cry: I was witnessing your birth into the world."

He is the real Razziel, Razziel Paritus. I owe him everything. I don't yet have the truth for which to thank him, but I am indebted to him for the knowledge that the truth of man is within man, that it is accessible to man.

However, he had not restored my memory to me. Maybe he could not salvage it from the hands of the torturers. The scraps of recollection that came to the surface were without coherence or solidity. My memory, my first true memory, remained hidden in secret corridors—it could make no connection with reality. I continued to know nothing about the years that had preceded my imprisonment. Who were my accusers? Who had risen in court to defend me? Who were my parents? Were they still alive? Did I have any friends? Brothers and sisters?

As time went by, I learned that I was in a Communist prison somewhere in a mountainous region of Romania. Why had they arrested me?

"Because of a word, perhaps, or a silent grimace," Razziel Paritus suggested, stroking his beard. "Or for something your parents were supposed to have done or said. In this country, denouncing people is a social duty, a moral imperative, a kind of state religion. It's also possible they arrested you for no reason at all. That your only crime is your innocence. Perhaps our executioners wanted to get their hands on it to test your resistance. There's no way of knowing. I believe what they've constructed here is a laboratory for psychological research. We are their guinea pigs, their human mice. For these people, torturing men's souls has become a science—and a passion too. They've evidently grasped that the real battlefield is in the human soul. What if they tried to play tricks with your memory in order to attack the thing it protects—your soul? Once they had probed it, analyzed it, dissected it, they could have refitted it in their own fashion and then emptied it, only to repeat the exercise with other people. Or maybe you were the one who rejected your memory in a defensive reflex, to protect your soul, just as the body sheds things that are foreign or harmful to it. In this day and age all hypotheses are possible."

He seemed to go off into a meditation that he was eager

to keep to himself and finished with his customary phrase: "One day you will know."

One day, one day. Which day? Where is this day hiding? Beneath what cloud? In what calendar? On what tree? What is it made of? Old Razziel Paritus would have liked to be able to answer these questions, but he was unable to do so. And I understood his powerlessness. "Here only the torturers have control of the solutions," he explained to me. "That, too, is part of their scientific experimentation. What they have at their disposal is the time they steal from their victims. At first, when they took power, they had only one word on their lips, the future. But in this prison what concerns them is the past. The torturers are ambitious: They want every part of our being. One day you will discover Dostoyevsky. In one of his novels a character exclaims, 'God is me; I am God.' That is the aim of the torturers: to become gods."

I must confess that at first I had difficulty in following my Master's thoughts. They seemed to me often obscure, complex, made up of words and, later, ideas whose sense and force were lost on me. Slowly, very slowly, I came to understand his language. In time my vocabulary was enriched. And my curiosity became greater. I began to measure the space that lies between the thought and the word, the memory of its source as well as its expression. I contrived to feel happy, happy to be alive, and to join my hopes with those of Razziel Paritus. Then, one evening, or one morning, as we were waiting for a meal that was late in coming, my poor victories vanished in an instant. The door opened and a jailer, with a paper in his hand, muttered, "Number

Two," and ordered me to get up and follow him. I tried to obey him but my body was not ready. I felt broken, defeated. It was old Paritus who helped me. He whispered in my ear, "Fear nothing; they'll soon bring you back. Whatever they say, whatever they do, remember my name, which from now on is yours. It must never leave you." Did he know something that had escaped me? Or was this just his way of reassuring me?

Like an automaton I followed the jailer along passageways lit by dirty gray lightbulbs. I went up staircases, down staircases, and up again. As I had lost the habit of walking, my legs hurt and I trembled at every step. I had the impression I was going around in circles; malevolent forces were swallowing me up, shaking me, dragging me in all directions. I felt giddy.

Finally, in front of a heavy door, the jailer gripped my arm and told me to stop. He knocked and called out some incomprehensible words. Thereupon the door was opened from inside and I was pushed into a kind of hospital ward. A man with a mustache and a woman with disheveled hair and a huge bosom seemed to be waiting for me. They both wore white coats. The jailer sat down in the corner while the man and the woman busied themselves in silence. Standing there motionless, I had a feeling of mounting panic. When would it erupt? Something strange, serious, dangerous was about to happen to me.

With a vague gesture, the man indicated that I should lie down on a long rectangular table covered in a more or less white sheet. Lying horizontally, I felt a thousand times more vulnerable. Were they going to hit me—mutilate me, perhaps? Interrogate me? What new confessions did they want to extract? Hammers began thudding in my skull. If only the woman with immense breasts, the man with the mustache, or even the jailer had said something, given an order, I would have felt somewhat reassured. But the silence grew denser. It was as if all three of them together were wrapping me in cotton wool, isolating me from the slightest noise, whether human or otherwise. I was turning into ash in the fire that blazed in my lungs; I was drowning in the blood that flowed in my veins. Toward what abyss was it carrying me? For some unknown reason I was terrified to breathe, and yet my rate of breathing speeded up. Why was the man in white walking with a silent tread toward the table where I lay stretched out? To stop my breathing because it disturbed him?

He leaned over my face and with his fingers forcibly closed my eyelids, as one does with a dead person. In order to cling to life I invoked the name and face of my cell companion. *Razziel, Razziel, come to my aid, help me to preserve the picture I have of you. Tell me what I must do to escape the silence of death.* My anguish modulated into panic and my panic into terror: They had just rolled back the right sleeve of my tattered jacket. Suddenly I felt a pain along the whole length of my arm, right up into my shoulder. Through half-open eyelids I saw the man in white with a syringe in his hand; he had injected a burning liquid into me. I had never known such agony. I was about to let out a howl but the woman with disheveled hair covered my mouth with her two hands and stifled it. Weakened, helpless, my will amputated, I sank into darkness.

I awoke in the cell. An iron bar was bearing down on my chest and on my brow. Was I dead? In my tomb? My arm began moving. Someone was shaking it. I summoned up my last reserves of energy to peer through closed eyelids and perceived a shadow leaning over me. I heard myself murmuring, "I don't remember anything, nothing." And the shadow answered softly, in barely audible tones, "Make an effort, my friend; just try, a little effort." An effort? My shattered body was not capable of such a thing. I too was no more than a shadow. The other persisted. "Tax your memory, just try; your life is at stake, and mine too." His voice calmed me, reassured me. I had an impulse to ask him, Who are you? But he asked me first. Involuntarily I whispered, "Razziel. Raz-zi-el." He repressed a little cry of joy. "Thank you, Lord! Well done, well done, my young friend! They didn't get you. Not quite! So we shall be able to begin again!"

And we did indeed begin our lessons again. My memory once more unlocked its bolted doors. My precious and unique friend passed on to me the things he knew. Things of the city, the outside world, the country. "The key, my dear fellow, the key, never forget, is in you, it *is* you; you are the key for me, as I am the key for you." And also: "It takes so little to hide the sun; if a scrap of paper is laid across your eyes, its light is eclipsed. But then another light wells up. This comes from your soul. And your soul is more powerful than all our torturers' instruments."

He recounted tragic episodes from the occupation. "The war is long since over, but nothing has changed; the dead, your grandparents, are still there. They call out to us. They judge us. Perhaps if they had been buried, things would be different. But they were not. And now it is for you to form a bond with them." He invoked a world inhabited by madmen, artists, and prophets who each in their own way reconstruct both the tower of Babel, which reached up to the heavens, and the heavens themselves. He told me stories from his own experience or drawn from books about God and his melancholy. About God's desire to make mortal man immortal. About the Messiah, who awaits a call in order to reveal himself to those who, against all odds, still await him. "All alone," said Paritus, "it is easy to live an upright life. But there are the others. God is God because he is alone." And also: "Feel free to fear solitude but not death. Everything is within us, death as well. We speak to death and it takes its time before answering us. It is death that gives life its human dimension. God is not human, for he is immortal." Whenever Paritus spoke, I felt the dawning of an emotion I would later call happiness. The happiness of not being alone. The happiness of no longer facing emptiness. The happiness of being present, of having a name: Razziel.

THE HUNCHBACK did not stir. At his screen he watched the prisoners, scrupulously noting their behavior, their reactions, their shifts of mood. It was his accustomed role: observing. That night, however, the Judge had decided to give him another task. The Hunchback was as yet unaware of this.

Her head bowed pensively, and with a diligent air, Claudia had started to cover a page with her delicate but illegible handwriting. She broke off for a moment, took her lipstick from her purse, hesitated over applying it, and put it away again. Bruce was amusing himself by drawing Spanish women dancing. Yoav, motionless, looked as if he were simply bored, but his mind was seething with energy as he pondered how to escape from this locked room controlled by dangerous madmen. George was putting questions to Razziel, who answered him slowly before questioning the archivist in his turn. All of them were being assailed by memories.

The Hunchback too. He remembered with terror the night he found himself in hell. Before that he had been a boy who was not especially good-looking and not really happy, but his father worked and his mother smiled as she laid the table. He liked almost everyone, and everyone adored him. At home, peace reigned supreme. At school, his fellows did not envy him the blessings of his childhood.

Then the accident happened. His father, a steady, cautious man, was driving their car when it collided with a truck. Who was at fault? The police investigation blamed it on the torrential rain. His parents and a baby a few months old were killed instantly. The Hunchback remembered his first encounter with the Judge. Severely injured and traumatized, the little boy had been taken to a special burn center, where for weeks he struggled to survive. He left the hospital handicapped, his face disfigured. Barely an adolescent, he was taken in by the Judge, who had no family. The Hunchback became his valet, his cook, his handyman, and his distorting mirror. Out of a deep sense of gratitude, he refused the Judge nothing. He tolerated his whims and oddities and took part in his "games." He had grasped that for the Judge life itself was merely a game—often cruel, sometimes funny.

One day the Judge invited in a passing beggar and made a deal with him: For one week the man would stop begging for alms and he, the Judge, would do so in his place. On another occasion he "married" a rather simpleminded elderly spinster and "renounced" her the next day, the Hunchback fulfilling the double function of sexton and mayor. But this latest game, with the five stranded travelers, went beyond anything the Hunchback had previously known. Let's hope it all ends well, he told himself. But how could he be certain? He tried to imagine what might happen next. The consequences. If he could have controlled the scenario, he would have pushed the participants into taking initiatives, stepping outside themselves. Let Bruce declare himself to be a builder of temples, let George begin to sing and dance. Let Razziel and Claudia have a quarrel or kiss; let them embrace one another fervently, passionately; let them do what he, the handicapped one, had never done. He had never known the experience of uniting his tormented body with that of a woman, any woman.

The Judge's severe voice rang out from a loudspeaker concealed in a corner of the room. He sounded just like a schoolmaster.

"It is late. No slacking, now! I've given you a game to play. Take it seriously. Get to work! Imagine you're actors. Act out your roles. Claudia, show them how it's done. Live the situation. It's serious. Tell yourselves you are really in danger. That Death is on the prowl. Confront and interrogate Death. What is it looking for beneath my roof? Surely it is preparing to choose a sacrificial victim. Which one of you will it be?"

As ever, when faced with danger, their first reaction is incredulity. "Is all this a dream or what? It can't be true. . . . It can't be happening to me, not now. . . . Not here in America!" Vastly different though they were, the five survivors reacted the same way. Surely, it was a prank . . . a charade in bad taste . . . a game for idiots or lunatics. Or maybe it *was* a psychodrama—yes, a therapy session, but one where it was the psychiatrist who needed help. The Judge had spoken of death. What did this mean? Was one of them really under threat? Had the Judge really "received" a message transmitted by supernatural powers? In any case, the whole situation was so absurdly improbable that it would be foolish to take it seriously. . . .

Suddenly Bruce rushed to the door, turned the handle—which resisted him—and thrust his shoulder against it with violence, then with a fury no longer under control. In vain. "We must get out of here!" he shouted. "Let's try the window! Let's smash it." But the two panes were made of a thick, unbreakable material. "That pervert! He's locked us in! We're like rats in a trap!"

Claudia tried to calm him. There was no sense in panicking. Sooner or later the Judge would return and order would be restored. He would laugh and so would they. She was interrupted by the voice of their host.

"Do not fritter away the time you have in rebelling against the Judgment. Be advised that it is not yet directed at any particular individual. For the moment Death is not in a hurry. Death takes its time, the choice has not yet been made. You have several hours at your disposal. For God's sake, use them as best you can!"

The survivors felt helpless against the fear that took them by the throat: So it wasn't a game?

Razziel was the first to react. "People in a similar situation in the Middle Ages would start to say their prayers. But we're no longer in the Middle Ages."

Claudia made an effort to overcome her distress. "All this is stupid. Out there the pilot, the crew, and the other passengers will soon notice our absence. They'll come looking for us. They'll alert the police."

Shrugging his shoulders, Yoav went further. "Remember, our destination is Israel. Our people there are used to critical situations. No doubt Mossad is in the picture already—"

The Judge's voice cut him off. "Don't be too sure of it. We're not at the cinema. Besides, not all movies have happy endings." After a silence, he saw fit to add, "The telephone is out of order. The weather forecast is bad. Two days and two nights will pass before contact can be made with those who have been more fortunate than you."

The Hunchback did not wait for any of the prisoners to react to this before intervening. "But miracles are always possible. I know a bit about that. They can happen when you least expect them. Do you want my opinion?"

Little by little, imperceptibly, the castaways felt well and truly trapped. Inexplicably, the voice of the Hunchback had changed; it was now marked by both warmth and uneasiness.

"I wish you no harm," he continued, "and here's my advice to you. Above all, don't panic; act as if it were really a game and play along with a good grace. It's pointless to resist the Judge; I speak from experience. Obey him, and he'll take account of it." Then, after a pause: "Look at me: I know I'm hunchbacked, but to keep shame and suffering at bay I sometimes tell myself I'm only playing the part of a hunchback. Do as I do. Isn't all human life a game in which the Lord himself makes the rules, in consultation with Satan?"

Claudia had a foolish impulse to quote Shakespeare—All the world's a stage. . . . Life's but a walking shadow, a poor player that struts and frets his hour upon the stage . . . a tale told by an idiot, full of sound and fury, signifying nothing—Razziel wanted to reply, No, my friend, God does not play games with his own creation. But both remained silent.

Curiously enough, some of the prisoners fell under the spell of the Hunchback's voice, as it came to them from outside the four walls of their room. They might have been ready to resist the Judge, but they allowed themselves to be persuaded by his servant. It was doubtless best to face up to the realities of the situation, however bizarre; maybe the game was becoming dangerous, but only insofar as it was a game. And since it was only a game, why get upset about it? In fact, why not give a merry laugh and say, OK, let's join in, like kids with nothing better to do. They certainly weren't going to take seriously the midnight fantasies of an unhinged madman who talked about death like an old acquaintance. What were they supposed to do, wail and tear their hair? Was everyone to draw up a balance sheet of his life? The only trouble was that the Judge held all the cards.

Yoav shook himself. Wary of bugs, he scribbled a few words on a piece of paper and showed it to his companions, one after another. *When this swine of a judge comes back, let's grab him. We'll turn the tables on him and make him our hostage.*

Some of them nodded: good idea, excellent idea. Only Razziel was not entirely convinced. The Judge and his accomplices were doubtless armed. Furthermore, everyone's agreeing to use violence didn't mean that they had, in fact, given up believing it was all simply a wager, a game, a stupid and puerile game, perhaps, but in essence harmless, and one that, at the end of the day, would be finished without injury to life or limb. On the other hand, if the Judge remained sole master of their fate and imposed his will on theirs, did not this already constitute his first victory? And then what would be the next, the death of one of them?

As for George, who knew he could have some influence on European history, no one would succeed in convincing him of it. He simply could not die before having shown the secret document to his colleague in Jerusalem. And Claudia, who had always been a survivor, with luck on her side since her earliest childhood, just knew she would live to see the man she loved—and because she loved him and he loved her, death would have no power over her. Razziel knew—yes, he *knew*—he could not die before meeting his friend, who was waiting to reveal to him the sources of his mutilated memory; afterward, yes, maybe, but not before. Yoav, thanks to his experience of war, was the only one to perceive the absurd as a possibility, if not a probability. In other words, even if it were only a game, a charade in bad taste, it was better to make profitable use of the time left to them to thwart the sadistic plans of this judge gone mad, knowing always that, whatever you may plan to do in advance the enemy may well have thought of first. As he pretended to write, Yoav concentrated his mind on what the intentions of their jailer might be.

Claudia laid down her pen in front of her and shook her head. I seem to be behaving like an idiot, she thought. Even if the Judge is really a judge and even if he's acting like a madman, what did he say before disappearing? That death is searching for prey. In other words: One of us is going to die. Just one. I have an eighty percent chance that it won't be me. Very well. Every time I walk through Greenwich Village to go to the theater I run greater risks.

In fact, while remaining skeptical, they were all asking themselves the same questions. How would the Judge choose the victim, by drawing lots? If not, what logic would he follow? Would he force them all to make the choice? Now very agitated, Bruce cried out, "Enough of these crazy calculations! They don't relate to anything! We've got to stop thinking about what that lunatic brain might inflict on us! We've got to find a way to escape!"

Easy to say. But how to achieve it, since the room was hermetically sealed? And how could they stop thinking about the threat that hung over them? An idea occurred to Razziel. That other prison I was in was even more closed, and yet I escaped it. Oh, Paritus, show me the way.

Yoav was remembering: He too had once encountered a strange man, as strange as the one Razziel had talked about—he seemed to have taken upon himself the mission to be the consoler of orphans. It was during the Yom Kippur War. The first battles had been disastrous for the Jewish State. The surprise attack by the Egyptians across the Suez Canal had cost the Israeli army such heavy losses that there was a risk the morale of the population—already at an all-time low—might collapse completely. The very existence of the newly formed state was in danger. Special teams, consisting of an army officer, a rabbi, and a social worker or psychologist, called on bereaved families to tell them they must go into mourning. When he lost one of his own soldiers, Yoav tried to carry out this mission himself. In words

simple and truthful, he would tell parents, wives, and children about the heroic way their loved ones had fought.

On each occasion, Yoav was followed by a nameless, ageless man. Tall, squarely built, with piercing eyes, he represented no authority, official or otherwise. What was he doing in those somber homes, heavy with distress, where you needed exceptional self-control not to burst into tears? On the sixth visit, or maybe the tenth, Yoav asked him.

"I'm on a mission," the strange visitor replied. "My purpose is to take charge of the future that our dead children leave behind. At midnight I go to the Wall and talk to the Lord. I implore him not to squander these young lives that have not yet been lived, nor these joys prematurely cut short, but to offer them to those who need them: the sick, the wounded, the invalids, people in despair. Sometimes my prayer is granted. Then the earth rejoices." One evening Yoav found him wandering downcast through the old city. "What has happened to you?" "I am in mourning." "Who is dead?" "Myself. I am dead." And, after a silence: "No, it's not me. It's my prayers that are dead. It's for them that I am in mourning."

The man disappeared into the night. Yoav never saw him again and never discovered his name.

The silence in the room, which was now bathed in a dim twilight, was unreal.

George remembered that in college his English teacher had once given his class an essay to write on the following theme: "You have twenty-four hours to live; how do you spend them?" Some students wrote about their heroic

dreams, others their erotic fantasies. Several of them composed a kind of will. The most brilliant of them wrote an essay on laughter. George himself, after several false starts, found himself incapable of giving any answer at all. He had ideas and knew how to express them, but they meant nothing to him. He could not contrive to grasp what it would signify to a man to be doing, saying, and seeing everything for the last time. How could one feel one was dying before actually dying? He decided to approach it obliquely: He did not speak about himself but quoted from and commented on the last words of the great historical, religious, and literary figures: Moses and Socrates, Goethe and Tolstoy, Giordano Bruno, Gertrude Stein. He did not earn a very good grade.

And now?

In his mind's eye he saw his grandfather: a piercing but concerned gaze, as always; shaggy hair, as if he had just emerged from the African bush or the Arizona desert; a permanently skeptical smile on his lips. He heard his nasal voice. "Do you understand the problem, my boy? It's insoluble. Science should be dedicated to preserving life, and man uses it as an instrument of death." A professor of nuclear physics, he had been recruited by Robert Oppenheimer to take part in the research project at Los Alamos. Like most of his colleagues, he carried with him a vague feeling of guilt at having contributed to the making of the atomic bomb. Yet he did not regret having collaborated on it. Like Albert Einstein, Leo Szilard, and Enrico Fermi, he knew the risk that the German scientists would get there first. They had to work quickly and well; hence the necessity to mobilize all wills, all talents, all governmental and academic resources. The survival of the free world depended on it.

What made George think about his grandfather that night? He adored him. He got on better with him than anyone else in the family. His grandfather was content to live with doubts, while his own son, George's father, fed upon certainties. The former radiated good humor, whereas the latter wore the severe mask of a preacher from dawn till dusk and well beyond. "Like Prometheus, you have robbed the gods of their secret," he would declaim, when the impulse came on him to speak. "They will take their revenge and punish us. If not tomorrow, then the day after." He would be silent for a moment and then add, "I, for one, hope I won't still be around when that happens."

So, Father, you are not around anymore. Nor you, Grandfather. What would you do if you were here, yes, in my shoes, or with me here? These twenty-four hours left to live, Grandfather: How would you use them? What would be your last will and testament? George would never have had the courage to put this question to his father. A rationalist, unsociable, his presence was burdensome. He was a hospital administrator who preferred the company of the patients to that of the doctors. Taciturn and depressive, he found it hard to conceal his frustration and suppressed anger in the face of the ills he struggled against. He would have liked his son to follow in his path and was disappointed to learn that, like his grandfather, he was more interested in an academic career.

And you, Father, George now pondered. What would you do? His father was dead—maybe from bitterness but surely from other causes too. George had been at his bedside. He would have liked to stroke his brow, to take his hand, but had not dared. His father discouraged all demonstrations of affection. How had he managed to tell his fiancée he loved her? Only his patients benefited from his gentleness. And there, as he lay dying, he had murmured, "George, my son. . . . The conversation we should have had, you and I, will never take place now." He had closed his eyes and given up his soul to God. And at that moment all the warmth went out of the world.

George felt a pang of anguish: Who would be at his own bedside when he died? He shut his eyes and had a vision of Pamela in the doorway of the office next to his. She signaled to him: "Shall I see you this evening?" Pamela had been pretty in her youth and, indeed, still was. Pamela, the embodiment of wisdom. Her innocent love. Pure affection, free of all bitterness and reproach.

His secret life.

At 1:30 A.M. the loudspeaker broadcast a CBS news bulletin: "The New York region is experiencing one of the worst snowstorms of the past few decades. A state of emergency has been declared. Airports are closed; roads are blocked. Tens of thousands of homes have lost electrical power. Churches, synagogues, and barracks have been converted into temporary shelters for the elderly and sick. Police reports indicate that the bad weather has already resulted in twelve deaths, and it is feared that the death toll will rise."

"You don't love me anymore," Lucien had said to her sadly.

Claudia remembered his sadness. It was not that Lucien never smiled; he smiled often, but it was his sadness that had won her heart. She had always loved his sadness; she saw it as being as much a gesture of trust as a cry for help. But this time it was different. Everything was different. He was frowning differently, he was suffering differently.

She had just told him she had decided to leave him. They were in the dining room. The table was set, the meal was ready. All of a sudden she caught sight of her reflection in the mirror and did not recognize herself. Her face was no longer hers. It was the face of a liar. I can't go on like this, she thought. It's too painful.

"You don't love me anymore," Lucien repeated, and his sorrow gave his mouth an especially sensual look.

"No, that's not the reason. But we ought to separate," said Claudia.

"Why?"

"It's the best thing. For you. For me."

Should she tell him she could no longer live with him because of the lie, because her own life had become a lie? What was the point? He would not understand. Explanations would no longer serve any purpose. It was too late for them.

Lucien gave a little joyless laugh that had nothing natural about it. "So that's it. Ten years of love and happiness, and it takes just one little sentence to end it all. What's happening to us, Claudia, if a few words can carry more weight than ten years of harmony and trust? What do those words hide? Have I—even in a dream—done something to offend you, humiliate you, hurt you?"

"No."

"So why do you want to leave me? You don't love me anymore? Not as much as before?"

Should she admit to him that her love for him had faded away, that she carried a dead love within her, and that it was not his fault but hers? Should she tell him about the wrong she had committed the previous week? Maybe he would forgive her for it, but she would never forgive herself.

Now they were silent. Nothing more to say? Lucien was thinking about his wife's wild and flamboyant beauty at night, the warmth that emanated from her body. Often, when they were making love, he would whisper in her ear, "This is the truth, my angel, this is the truth about you and me." But Claudia, for her part, would be thinking: There is no longer any truth; truth itself is a lie. Had she really ever loved Lucien? She used to think so in the old days. Now she was no longer sure. She told herself that she had never given herself to him entirely. One part of her was not involved, remained at a distance, like an observer with dulled senses. When love dies you forget the fire that made it sing.

Remembering that evening, thinking about that last conversation, which had turned out to be so short, Claudia asked herself, Which is better, truth that is a lie or the lie that is truth? An observation of Gertrude Stein's, when she was dying, came into her mind: "There is no answer. There never was an answer. There never will be an answer. And maybe that is the answer." Now, in this snowbound prison, she rebelled against this fatalism. To favor questions is one thing, but to deny the possibility of all answers is quite another. And for Claudia, since her break with Lucien, that answer had finally come to exist. It had a name, a face, a face like no other; all the beauty of the world and all its strength could be read in it; all the imagination and fervor of the muses radiated forth from it. David. Yes, the answer was called David. And he was waiting for her. And she would find him again. And they would show the world that the heart can be surprised and that love is not necessarily tragic in essence.

Bruce Schwarz stopped pacing up and down the room. "I think I've got it!" he exclaimed.

"What have you got?" Claudia asked.

George stopped writing and looked up. Razziel, too, looked at Bruce with curiosity; his thick lower lip was trembling strangely.

"Yes, it's clear now," said Bruce. "These guys must be terrorists."

"Terrorists?" George said in amazement.

"Hostage takers."

"How could kidnapping us serve their purposes?"

"Who knows? Maybe they want to use us to obtain a ransom or to get prisoners released—here, in Saudi Arabia, or in Israel—you see what I'm talking about?"

For a moment there was silence, as the import of these words bore down on the prisoners with its burden of uncertainty. Visions of victims of recent assassination attempts arose before their eyes, as if seeking revenge.

Hostile to everything Bruce said, Claudia put down her pen and rejected his theory with contempt. "That's a bit farfetched! How could the Judge and his accomplices have foreseen first the snowstorm and then that our plane was going to land near this village?"

Impeccable logic, thought Razziel. Terrorists can manipulate public opinion but not the weather.

"They could have prepared everything a long time in advance," Bruce replied. "Then all they had to do was to wait for the moment when all the necessary conditions came together."

"It's possible," George said. "Yes, what you say is possible. But in that case our situation would be even more hopeless."

"Tragic, but not serious, as they used to say," said Bruce, with bitter irony.

"Terrorists are always serious," said George. "Too serious, even."

He embarked on a historical account of terrorism. The Russian nihilists, the anticzarist revolutionaries—oh, it was different in the old days. A hundred years ago they never attacked children or civilians. He quoted Dostoyevsky and Camus. He was just getting ready to mention some "sensational" texts he had found in the archives when Bruce stopped him.

"That's enough, professor. We'll listen to you some other time, but not now."

Nevertheless, the debate continued. How can one explain the attraction terror holds for some minds—and why for intellectuals? Is it a longing for power? The desire to make an impact with actions rather than words? Maybe for romantic motives? In a totalitarian and terrorist regime, man is no longer a unique being with infinite possibilities and limitless choices but a number, a puppet, with just this difference—numbers and puppets are not susceptible to fear.

. . .

The "hostages" began to believe it. Bruce's theory had the advantage of explaining a lot of things: the mutation of their rescue into an incarceration, the Judge's interrogation, his seeking to learn everything about their private lives, his threats. But if they really were among terrorists, their identity had yet to be discovered. Palestinians? Abu Nidal's gang? Possible. After all, the plane had been headed for Israel. But the objections made a moment before remained valid: How could terrorists have foreseen the weather and the forced landing on a deserted airstrip near this isolated house? Another possibility: The Judge and his men might be part of a network of Brazilian gangsters. In Rio and São Paulo, kidnappings were common, often followed by ransom demands. If this was the case, they should be offering a large sum of money. But to whom? To the Judge? To the Hunchback? And how much? Only Bruce had money on him: more than $5,000. "I have my checkbook with me," said Claudia. "But I imagine terrorists prefer cash." But what if they were Irish nationalists? Members of Sinn Fein? Should they offer to intervene politically? None of the five had connections in high governmental spheres. Statements to the press? Their authority in this field was nil. Such is the power of autosuggestion, thought Razziel. We're reacting as if the imagined situation were true. He himself found it hard to believe. Something did not fit. A real terrorist doesn't act the part of a judge but that of a terrorist, so what was the Judge playing at?

"If we're hostages," observed Claudia, looking at Razziel, "and if our jailers are terrorists, we're finished. We've seen their leader's face. He can't run the risk of letting us go free."

Razziel nodded. Why did Claudia, so attractive, so sure of herself, address her remarks to him? Was she looking for a protector, an ally? Was she attributing to him a strength that he himself had no inkling of? An intelligence capable of solving insoluble problems? Razziel remembered that, when airplanes were hijacked, the Palestinian terrorists separated the Jews from their fellow travelers. What if that were to happen here too? Were Yoav and he the only Jews? What about Bruce Schwarz? And the archivist, how would he react? And Claudia?

"For the love of heaven," yelled Bruce, his anger rising and falling in successive waves, "we must do something! Whether it's a game or not, once and for all we must get out of this goddamned whorehouse of a prison!"

He twisted his red scarf and made it into a running knot, as if he intended to strangle the Judge.

"I just love it when you say 'once and for all,' " replied Claudia. "But would you care to explain how you propose to set about knocking down these walls and making the storm abate?" She turned to Yoav. "And you, brave officer of an invincible army, what do *you* think? What do *you* plan to do? Do you have a plan for liberating us from this prison? Because we needn't kid ourselves any longer. We're sure as hell in prison."

The word *prison* on the young woman's lips made Razziel shiver. He knew prison.

"Miracles can happen, according to the Hunchback," said Yoav.

"When soldiers start talking about miracles it's a bad sign," Claudia said.

"Are you telling us to get down on our knees and pray?" said Bruce furiously.

"There are also human miracles," remarked Razziel, "made by men for men."

Bruce gestured despairingly. "He's off his head."

"Terrorists are men, too," said Claudia. "They're vulnerable. And mortal, thank God."

Yoav leaned toward her and whispered in her ear. "Right now the best thing to do is wait. Wait for the Judge to make the next move. Sooner or later he'll make a mistake. If he comes back alone we'll take him prisoner."

Meanwhile, George went on writing meticulously, with a serious air, as if he were drawing up his will.

Once more it was the Hunchback who brought the hot tea. Suddenly all eyes were focused on him. Was he a terrorist too? Razziel stared at his disfigured face, Claudia at his hands. What part did this misshapen man have to play in the Judge's scheme? Bruce asked him if it was still snowing, George asked if he could have coffee instead of tea, and Yoav asked if the Judge would come back soon. Razziel took refuge in silence.

"Well, now," said the Hunchback, without addressing anyone in particular, "what do you make of all this? And of the Judge? And of his judgment? Which one of you will sacrifice himself for the sake of your holy community? For you do form a community now, don't you?"

"We might choose you," joked Bruce.

A look of alarm, quickly dissipated, appeared in the Hunchback's eyes: "No, not me. I'm part of the court."

"How about the Judge?"

"Judges survive executions. That's the law."

Bruce persisted with his questions; the presence of the Hunchback among the hostages could only be useful to them. With a bit of luck he might let slip some useful scraps of information about the life, character, and personality of the Judge. Bruce was right; the Hunchback began confiding expansively.

"The Judge? What can I say about him? Well, I don't know very much myself. They say his wife and daughter were brutally raped and murdered. It's best not to say how. . . . They say so many things here in the village. Everyone has some particular odd thing to relate about my master, this man of mystery. They never caught up with the murderer. Was he a prowler looking for shelter? A drug addict with withdrawal symptoms? A sex-starved prisoner on the run? They say his daughter was mentally sick. Oh, yes, there's plenty of things they say, plenty of things. Some folk think the Judge spent years tracking down the murderer and finally caught him. He may even have killed him with his bare hands. But there's no proof."

He looked at Claudia and blushed. Did the others notice? He felt at a loss. He wanted to add something, warm words addressed to her alone. But they stuck in his throat. He experienced a powerful urge to laugh, to weep, to leap in the air. It had just dawned on him that he was in love with her, and that his love was rare, unique. The whole world had only been created for this moment, for this encounter, so that he, sole survivor of his family, might love this woman. Even if she did not love him, what mattered was that he loved her; he was capable of feeling love and perhaps worthy of inspiring it. He felt a warm glow; he was becoming a man.

A memory rose in him. He's going to the drugstore. The pharmacist is away. His wife, her hair untidy, her eyes wild, stares at him, as always, in a way that makes him uneasy. "We're alone at last," she says, moistening her lips with her tongue. "We're going to make love, my little Hunchback. Do you want to? They say it brings good luck." He feels the blood coursing faster through his veins and a fire burning his eyes. What can he do to breathe normally? He experiences something unknown that resembles thirst. As good luck—or bad luck—would have it, a customer appears. The pharmacist's wife laughs, hands a tube of something or other to the Hunchback, and pays him no further attention. And the Hunchback runs away like a thief after his first failed robbery.

"Your judge," said Bruce. "You're very attached to him, aren't you?"

"I'm devoted to him. I owe him my life. He's a curious character."

"So are you. You're a curious character."

"It's not surprising. We have a lot of memories in common."

"Tell me about them?"

"It's for him to tell you. I don't have the right."

"And he does?" asked Bruce.

"He has all the rights. He's like God."

"Like God in the suffering he metes out?"

"In the fear he inspires."

"Is he religious?"

"Yes, he is. He has his own religion. It's awesome."

"What are you to him?" asked Bruce.

"It's for him to tell you."

"What is he to you?"

"A master. A power. A divinity."

"Do you do everything he tells you?"

"Everything."

"Without argument?"

"You don't argue with the Judge."

"So you're his slave?"

The Hunchback bowed his deformed head. "Yes, I'm his slave." And two tiny tears began to trickle down his fire-scarred cheeks.

IS IT MY fate that I cannot love you anymore? That you no longer love me? That I must live far away from your grave in repentance and without hope of expiation? Father, forgive me. Yesterday at the cemetery I asked your forgiveness. I'm thirty-five, and I need to know you're reconciled to my future. What unseen road were you following when you were my age?

Standing before the mirror, Yoav had stared at his face without recognizing it. Was it the beard? Carmela thought it made him look uglier but Yoav had refused to shave it off during the week of mourning. In fact, he disliked it as well. It reminded him of his commando operations; on his return he was always bearded.

He had shaved yesterday morning but looked pretty awful already. I've changed, he thought. I won't change anymore. No more chasing the thrill of nocturnal confrontations with the enemy. Shmulik keeps coming back to me bloody and open-mouthed. I'm past all desires; too many dead people dwell within me.

Yoav no longer wanted to lose himself in the memory of friends now dead and in his dread of the unknown.

You are in my thoughts, Father, but I no longer want to die in order to meet up with you again in the hereafter. Carmela is the only person who helps me in my struggle to conquer fear and grief and find some meaning to the few weeks or months that are left for me to live. Is this enough? Can one live in a world inhabited by just one person? Forgive my pessimism, Father, but whose fault is it? Mine alone? And what is this *me* we are talking about? Does this *me* grow old? Does it on occasion tell lies, disguise itself, hide itself? What will happen to this *me* when I'm no longer here, when I'm nothing? You, Father, who loved philosophy so much, will you help me to direct my steps toward the light and not toward the darkness? You, who were attracted by the quest of the mystics, will you give me your hand so it may burn at their touch?

You, who in your own way believed in miracles, can you not make one happen for me now? That's what I need in order to breathe the freedom you bequeathed to me when you died. "Loving the unexpected," you used to say, "is to define yourself in relation to miracles." It was one year after you had left the army. You began to study the sacred texts you had put aside in your youth. And it was when you were questioning me about the commando's life I was just beginning to lead that you used the word *miracle*. You saw the look of surprise on my face. And you explained to me the connection between the unexpected and the miraculous.

Did I ever manage to convey to you, Father, the depth of

my attachment to you? When you were present, sometimes you weighed heavy on me. Now that you're gone, I miss you all the time. Why did I feel the need to make you suffer?

I'm thirty-five, Father, and I still have much to learn and so little to offer. Except to Carmela: To her I offer my future happiness and my past joys. But between you and me, it's too late. You can never receive the joy and pride a son owes his father.

Yoav had another memory linked to his father's death.

There had been a knock at the door of the house. Yoav did not stir. He had no desire to see anyone. During a period of mourning everyone has the right to live as he wishes. And anyway, the door was open. Such is the custom. During the week following the funeral the door is not locked. Anyone can come in to offer you words of comfort by extolling the virtues of the deceased. The knocking came again. It must be Rivka, the cleaner, Yoav thought wearily. Rivka is polite. Yes, that's it. Rivka has always been courteous. Well brought up. Excellent education. Good manners. She's irritating, Rivka, always eager to come out with an appropriate remark. Now she's going to tell me how sad she is for me. And that I must try to overcome my grief. Right, let her come in.

But it was not Rivka. Dressed in black, a man who was still young—in his forties?—stood on the threshold. A Hasid? His face reflected sadness, his eyes melancholy.

"I saw you at the cemetery yesterday," said the visitor.

"Right," said Yoav.

"I knew your father."

Yoav almost replied, I didn't, but he checked himself. The visitor seemed devoid of malice.

"I owe your father a great deal," said the visitor.

Yoav could not stop himself thinking, More than I? As custom dictated, he went and sat on his stool and waited for the Hasid to seat himself on a chair facing him.

"I was living through difficult times," said the visitor. "It was your father who saved me. His appearance in my life was nothing short of miraculous."

Fine, thought Yoav. This one too. He's going to bore me with the stories of miracles my father served up to his listeners' delight.

"There were many people at his funeral," added the visitor. "Your father was a very popular man. He loved you very much, I'm sure of that. And you—you loved him, didn't you?"

Impelled by an obscure fear, Yoav longed to get up and chase the intruder away. Let him be gone with his tedious tales: Let him clear off, the sooner the better. But he remained sitting there. In the Hasid's presence he felt more alone than ever. Nothing else existed beyond his solitude. Then, without his knowing why, welling up from the depths of his being, tears rose to his eyes. He did not want to weep, but he was weeping. He wanted to blow his nose and wipe his eyes, but his hands would not obey him. No part of him obeyed him. His tears flowed and did not stop flowing. What's happening to me, for God's sake, Yoav asked himself. What's happening to make me cry like this?

"Weeping is a miracle too," said the visitor.

Amazed, Yoav raised his head and looked at him. But it

was his father he saw. And his father was making signs to him that he did not understand.

One morning, six months after his father's death, Yoav took a call from his doctor at Tel-Hashomer military hospital.

"I'd like to see you."

"Is it urgent?"

"Fairly urgent."

"My tests?"

"Come over. I'm waiting for you."

Yoav leaped into his car. Carmela was still asleep; they had spent a long evening with an American army officer on an official visit who had not returned to his hotel until two o'clock in the morning.

Carmela was not aware that his health was deteriorating. What was the use of upsetting her? So as not to worry her, he had not told her about his most recent visits to the doctor, the extensive tests.

"Yoav," said Dr. Schreiber, "how long have we known one another?"

"Ten years. Maybe twelve."

"Fifteen."

Yoav looked him in the eye. "These preliminaries make it sound as if you have bad news for me. Am I wrong?"

"No, Yoav."

"What I've got is as serious as that."

"It's pretty serious."

"Incurable? Tell me everything. I can take the truth, you know that, don't you?"

"Yes, I know."

"So what is it?"

"A tumor. In the brain. Rare. Very rare. In principle it's inoperable."

Yoav took a deep breath. "How many years do you give me?"

"Two. Three. Maybe less. It all depends on the treatment. In certain cases the side-effects are intolerable. And even if treatment is successful, it only alleviates the condition. It doesn't cure it."

They spoke for a long time. They were friends, comrades in arms; they had lived through a lot.

"But there's one thing we could try," said Dr. Schreiber.

"What's that?"

"At Sloan-Kettering, a cancer research center in New York—I know one of the doctors. He's good. Go and see him. Tell him I sent you."

Yoav went home and found Carmela in the kitchen.

"You went off without drinking your coffee."

He made her sit down opposite him, took her two hands and kissed them, and gave her a heavily edited account of his conversation with Dr. Schreiber. Carmela, her eyes open wide, stared at him with grief-struck intensity. But she shed no tears. She showed no emotion. She even tried to smile.

"Right, we'll go to America. I always wanted to see New York in the fall."

"And if it goes on into the winter?"

"So much the better. I've never seen snow in my life."

How can one describe their weeks together in America? Every day, every night, their struggle against the enemy brought them closer to one another. But Carmela, exhausted, was growing visibly thinner. She spoke less, rarely laughed.

She went back to Israel before him to prepare for his return.

Claudia was thinking about how she had split up with Lucien. Where was he at this moment? Doubtless in his overheated apartment. Did he still love her? And she, had she ever really loved him, ever truly been in love with him, loved him as she now loved David?

For ten years the two of them, still young, had lived in a harmony that was at once stimulating and soothing. Even when they disagreed about the merits of a concert (she preferred Schubert to Brahms) or the worth of a promise made by a politician (she was a Democrat, he a Republican), they found fascination and enrichment in the way their opinions differed. Each one helped the other to reach out farther, to banish the malevolent demons that lie in wait for all couples. Certainly their patience sometimes ran out, they lost their tempers, but that did not affect their love, based as it was as much on mutual respect as on the passion they nourished for one another. Now she knew it had not been love—not quite love—just something that had resembled love.

A chance incident at the theater was the trigger.

Why had she yielded to temptation that evening? Out of pity for poor Bernard Fogelman, the unfortunate director who had just been humiliated in front of his actors? They were rehearsing an excellent play, a first play by a young author, in which a couple only finds fulfillment by tearing each other apart; happiness eludes them, cruelty and ugliness bring them closer together. A stupid and pointless argument had broken out between Bernard and Jacqueline—magnificent Jacqueline, as she liked people to call her. It arose from a scene in which she had insisted that her lover abase himself before her, so she could raise him up and restore to him his dignity as a man. Bernard had wanted her to be humbler, more malleable at the start of her long speech, while she insisted on remaining imperious and dominating throughout. At one point, Bernard had cried out, "But don't you see that, in spite of all that makes them argue, these two characters still love each other? They love each other even when they fight, possibly *because* they fight! Is that so hard for you to understand?" And Jacqueline had replied to him spitefully, without raising her voice, "You talk of love but you don't know a goddamned thing about it. Is it so hard for you to stop getting in my face? I don't need advice from eunuchs."

Bernard was shaken by her words. He turned pale, swallowed, and said nothing. As he looked at the actress, he saw she had dropped her mask and was regarding him with open hostility—and, worse still, as a stranger. He spoke very quietly. "OK. I see that humiliating someone is for you a way of loving him. I can't argue with that." Whereupon the other actor in the scene protested angrily, "Say, who's the director here, you or her? I don't see my character that way at all. Yes, I can be humiliated by love—but not on a whim!" "No one asked your opinion!" Jacqueline yelled.

With a helpless gesture, Bernard had stopped the rehearsal and called it a day. Dumbfounded and embarrassed, the actors went home and Bernard shut himself in his dressing room at the theater. He took a long time to answer when Claudia knocked on the door.

"I don't want to talk," he said.

"But I do," said Claudia.

She had never seen him look so lost, so dejected, he who thrived on directing, giving orders, getting what he wanted.

"I knew she was vain and arrogant," said Claudia, "but not to that extent. It beats me why she got mad at you, unless—"

"Unless what?"

"Unless you two are having an affair."

"You're crazy."

"Maybe, but not stupid. That tantrum of hers suggested a kind of bitter intimacy. Maybe disappointed love. She sounded like an unsatisfied woman who has some claim on you."

Bernard laughed out loud: a nervous, destructive, sick laughter. "For God's sake, do you really think she's my lover? You're crazy, I tell you." And he began crying. "I've never slept with her," he said, after a moment.

Claudia was on the brink of saying, but you'd have liked to. In other words, you're in love with her, and she knows it.

Bernard was shaking his head. "Look, I've never slept with her. Nor with any woman. I've never even tried."

Is he gay? Claudia wondered. Surely not. Robust, virile, he was a man made to love women. Bernard answered her unspoken question.

"I'm not gay, you know. I've never had an affair with a man. But women just don't like me. I guess I'm worthless; nobody wants me."

Claudia walked over to him. This man, neither young

nor old, was someone she admired for his talent and his integrity. He sat with his head in his hands, racked by sobs. Nothing was left of his authority, his charisma. His sacred fire, his enthusiasm, his passion were extinguished. All that because he had never known a woman's body? That's stupid, she said to herself; it makes no sense. And she stroked his tousled hair, covered his face with light, delicate kisses, and whispered kind, soothing words . . . and in the end proved him to be a man.

But she did not love him. And she no longer loved Lucien. Without a love of her own, she was ready to meet David.

Bruce Schwarz felt a pang of anxiety: Even if it was a game, he did not want to die without once more seeing Stacy, the young student in psychiatry—without having explained to her the reasons why he kept going off the deep end; without begging her forgiveness for his shameful conduct, toward her and toward women in general. If I die, he wondered, will my death be an expiation? Will all my sins be washed away?

In fact, for more than a year, ever since he had met Stacy, Bruce had been traveling around the world, looking for all the women he had deceived, scorned, and abandoned as if he needed their understanding, their forgiveness. There were a lot of them: young and not so young, intellectuals and artists, rich heiresses and poor orphans, beautiful women and homely ones. He had not been choosy. Was he nostalgic for some love affair in his youth, some woman who had scorned him?

Driven by irrational and perhaps subconscious forces, he had considered it his duty to seduce women, one after another, to conquer them, to keep them for a time before casting them aside, with the excuse that he was not good enough for them. They deserved someone more mature, he said, more sensitive, more moral: in a word, more human. A sweet talker, he had great faith in his powers of persuasion. He believed he was sufficiently convincing to spare them suffering. He was wrong, of course. Even those who hid their despair from him would shut themselves away to weep at home where they ran no risk of being disturbed. Deep down, he knew this but, cravenly, he would manage to forget. Affairs were for him like pages to be turned: The new one makes the preceding ones disappear.

Until the day of awakening. Having fallen in love, body and soul, he first suffered the pangs of rejection. The young woman, Stacy, was neither more beautiful nor more attractive than the others. But in his eyes she was different, singular, unique. The sober elegance with which she dressed; the way she compressed her lips when she was thinking; her proud carriage as she walked down the street, upright and self-confident; her dark eyes, where all the suns in the world took fire and faded in each of her glances. Stacy reproached him for his lack of faith, for his lack of contact with God. She believed in God. Without God, life makes little sense, she would say. For her, human love could not be dissociated from the love of God. "And the other way around?" Bruce asked her mischievously. "Yes," she replied gravely. He tried in vain to shake her convictions. She remained inflexible. It was Stacy who had given him the red scarf. He wore it always, even in summer.

How easy it had been to hoodwink the others. . . . Bruce still remembered his first conquest with a pride that now did not quite tally with the feelings that were so new to him: remorse and anguish.

"Oh, you poor man," Razziel's strange friend and Master, old Paritus, the sad, mocking mystic, had cried out to him in a dream. "You and your dreams of making the Redeemer come. You make me laugh. Do you really think he is still alive? Do you really think he'll appear one day, just like that, to please you? Seriously, my boy, I knew you were naïve and mad, but not to that extent. Can it be that you long to be a prophet too? Do you really think that the Savior we have been waiting for so long will materialize out of thin air tomorrow or next year to bring you his light and grace? Don't be stupid. Stop waiting for the end. We've passed it already. The end is behind us. The Redeemer is not going to come now. And if he ever comes he'll need our pity more than we need his. Anyway, he's lost all his powers, believe you me. I know what I'm talking about. He's taken too long to get here. He's missed his opportunity, let it slip through his fingers. The artist has forgotten his art, and now he's nothing anymore. He's just a poor soul, like you or like me, which comes to the same thing."

Razziel had woken that day with a start, oppressed by a feeling of panic. What was this rock crushing him from inside? He recalled the true Paritus, the melancholy dispenser of consolation. Why is he grinning now? Why and how long has he been making fun of me? When he laughs, one half of his face lights up and the other half remains dark, plunged in shadow. O wonderful Paritus! thought Razziel. He pursues me even in my sleep. Will he help me recover my lost memories? Is he my unique salvation? But what if he were my utter downfall instead?

For years now Razziel has been pursuing Paritus, searching for him. After their release from prison he had met him several times. Once in Paris, among the homeless people beside the Seine. Once in a lecture hall at Oxford University. And a third time on the morning of Yom Kippur at the court of the Rebbe of Kamenets in Brooklyn, reading from the book of Jonah. Most of the time Paritus was nowhere to be found. On each occasion when Razziel thought he had unmasked him, or at least located him, he vanished once more—so often that Razziel felt he now knew him not nearly as well as in the old days. Had he really lived in the fifteenth century? Had he really encountered Rabbi David ben Gdalya beside the Wall in Jerusalem? And why had he spoken of meeting Samuel Saportas, the famous repentant heretic, who came to the Holy Land to show that for him nothing was sacred? And why had Paritus spoken of redemption just now in Razziel's dream?

Automatically, his arm reached out, searching for Kali, but encountered only emptiness. How long had the only woman in his life been dead? Lying on his right side, Razziel knew he ought to get up, his duties awaited him at the yeshiva, but he had no desire to do so. Razziel was no longer the same man. He still knew the goal but not the road that led to it. Should he begin a new day, only to go to bed again at the end of it? What was the point? Why not lie in bed until tomorrow? Razziel felt tired, heavy. The smallest movement cost him considerable effort. Even his mind was sluggish; it was impossible to drag it from its starting point and launch it in pursuit of imaginary friends or enemies. His depression was pushing him toward the abyss. Oblivion would be a blessing. Can I be dead? he wondered. What's certain is that someone has died within me. Who? The man I was? The man I might have been?

Razziel shook himself. Outside, a gray dawn had appeared. Was it an autumn day or a day in spring? Would it bring happiness or sorrow? What did it matter? It would be a day like any other. Words spoken, words held back. Children hungry, people betrayed. Anonymous visitors. Handshakes, smiles, courtesies. A meeting with . . . with whom? What if he did not go to it? Better still, what if he ceased doing anything? I'm fifty. What if I threw in the towel, simply announced that I've had enough? So long, students: Someone else will guide you toward the heights. So long, future masters: Don't follow my example. So long, everybody: good night. And as for all the rest, go home, with all your fantasies and your weaknesses, your wives and mistresses. This player no longer wishes to entertain you. This player is content to have no more desires.

Was I nothing but an actor? Razziel wondered, nothing more? Was I simply wearing different masks: the prodigal son, diligent student, husband, pilgrim? And now? The last mask, Paritus used to say, is the one death lays on your face, what's more, there is a touch of death on all faces. At that, Razziel became irritated: Get away, you old learned devil! You're disturbing me; you're irritating me. What a bore you are! Why don't you go annoy someone else for a change? I need some respite.

It was true: Razziel needed a rest. Like a man who has lived too hard, endured too much, he deserved to be left in peace. To find his bearings. To renew himself. Razziel was suffocating. Caught in a cold and comfortless stranglehold, he felt he was a prisoner without knowing whose. But he knew why. He had committed grave errors. He was guilty of having entered the orchard of forbidden knowledge. Guilty in the eyes of God and men, guilty toward his father—whom he knew no longer, or did not know as yet—and above all guilty of having wasted a life: his own.

Once upon a time, everything was simple. There was an established order that all creation respected. The sun shone in summer, and in winter the snow fell softly and covered everything. You got up in the morning, you spent the day studying, praying, working, eating, and in the evening you went to bed.

Once upon a time. . . .

Did Razziel like sleeping when he was little? Was slumber for him a way of dying? Was he afraid of never waking up? When he opened his eyes in the morning did he quickly cover his head with his *kipa* to recite the first prayer of the day, *Thank you, for having rendered my soul unto me, O God*? And later on did he say, *The soul you have given me is pure; it is you who have created it; it is you who have breathed it into me; it is unto you that I will surrender it*?

Razziel had always loved these prayers. They reassured

him. As long as he was praying, nothing bad could befall him. If someone had asked him what prayer meant to him, he would have replied: a shelter and a defense, a protection against rough winds and the wickedness of man.

The heretic Samuel Saportas detested prayer. He considered it to be inextricably linked with flattery. "He who prays, lies," he said, "and he who prays not, also lies. That is the tragedy of human life: man always lives a lie."

Well, perhaps he's not wrong, thought Razziel. At any rate not totally wrong. The ones who don't lie are the madmen, God's madmen.

Razziel had a great affection for these inspired madmen, these fugitive prophets, these dreamers of eternity; their rich imagination nourished his own. All those madmen on the street in his district—and those in Brooklyn and Manhattan too—they all knew his address. The gentle and the violent; the young, cursing their youth; the old, dreading their own decay—they would write to him or turn up at his yeshiva out of the blue, one fine morning or in the middle of the night, to confide in him or simply to offer him the fruits of their imagination. Between lessons Razziel would welcome them and listen to them patiently, intently, without ever getting annoyed, letting each of them feel he was expected, that his presence mattered, and what he had to say was appreciated.

In the beginning, Kali did not understand. "You're too available," she reproached him. "Too accommodating. Too generous with your time. Absolutely everybody takes the liberty of stealing it from you. Don't you think you ought to be a little more discriminating?" By way of a reply, he quoted to her from Paritus: "God gives to those who give of themselves. How can I withhold myself from people who have nothing?" Kali could not be angry with him for long. "But if Father did the same thing with his customers or his bank account he would have been ruined long ago," she told him gently.

Was Kali right? Razziel asked himself now. Have I paid too much attention to strangers and not enough to my own family? What has become of them? No doubt they despise me. And the fact that my memories run away from me and reject me is proof. What is harder to bear, the shattered memory of a beloved wife or the silent reproach of the child within me?

As on the day of Yom Kippur, Razziel examined his life as a man. What have I done that I should not have done? What errors have I committed? When and where have I been unjust? The fifty years I have lived, will I see them slide into the hungry, yawning abyss? Will no trace of them or of myself remain? Where is Paritus in all this? And where is God? Will you, Lord, really allow everything that I have tried to write in your book, in your memory, to be erased?

Outside, a voice can be heard. "Hurry. The service is about to begin."

"I'm coming, Father," replies a young voice.

The pious Jews of Brooklyn woke early, as they did every morning. In accordance with the Lord's sacred injunction, each went to his place of worship to repeat the prayers composed by the Ancient Sages with future generations in mind.

Razziel, too, should have got up, even earlier than everyone else. But that morning he did not have the strength:

Kali's absence weighed too heavily. He stayed in bed a moment longer, contemplating through half-closed eyelids the faces that had peopled his fragmented past; he spoke to them, but none of them replied.

"So are you coming?" repeated the same voice, becoming impatient.

"I'm coming, I'm coming!"

"Hurry up! You could make an effort, after all! So God is waiting for you and you're late? Aren't you ashamed to keep God waiting?"

The voice—a little boy's?—is lost in the noise of the street, but within himself it is Razziel who replies: Yes. I'm ashamed.

The center that Razziel directed was officially a yeshiva for "outstanding students." People went there to study what is taught in all Talmudic schools: how to interpret biblical texts, to search for the deeper meanings of the midrashic commentaries; how to understand the laws, both simple and complex, concerning the commerce between men and their relationships with the surrounding world, sacred or profane. Razziel had appointed three masters to assist the pupils in grappling with the most impenetrable passages. He himself helped the final-year students to discover the glories of the Zohar; mysticism was his reserved, exclusive field. He taught late into the evening, until almost midnight: the mysteries of the Beginning; the secret of the presence of God within time; the significance of the *klipot,* or parings, that would explain the presence of evil in the creation; the agonizing questions connected with the promised coming of the Messiah. All these Aramaic texts that are meant to be explored and communicated in small groups, Razziel would translate for his pupils, chanting in a low voice in the half-light. Sometimes they would be disturbed by a stranger bursting into the little house of study asking for something to eat or drink or just some attention, a human gesture. Calmly, Razziel would rise and invite him to go with him into the next room, where his needs would be met. At the beginning, his pupils did not hide their astonishment. And once more he would quote one of Paritus's sayings: "Helping a man to overcome his sadness is more important than understanding the ultimate will of the Lord." And he told them the story of Rebbe Levi Itzhak of Berditchev, who commanded his disciples to spend forty days and forty nights preparing to meet him at a secret spot in the forest. There they were to force God's hand and precipitate the coming of the Messiah. Excited, stimulated by this challenge, they all set about purifying themselves, body and soul: They took no food (except on the Sabbath) other than dry bread and water. They spent their nights lamenting the destruction of the Temple and the exile of the Shekinah. They did all that was necessary to be ready and worthy of their mission. The awesome day arrived. They all met in the forest, equipped with their prayer books and their ritual shawls—all except for their Master. Where could he be? He only appeared after several hours.

"I know I have disappointed you," he told them. "How can I justify my late arrival? At least let me explain it to you. On my way here I passed a house where an infant was crying. I knocked at the door; there was no one with the child. No doubt the parents had had to go out. So was I to go away too? And leave an infant alone with his fear, alone with his hunger? I approached the cradle and soothed the child. Do you understand? When a child is crying, the Messiah can wait."

After that, the pupils were no longer surprised whenever Razziel interrupted his teaching to welcome a starving beggar or a widow in mourning. Who knows? Maybe they were messengers.

For his first lesson, Razziel had quoted Paritus:

> In the beginning, tradition tells us, was the word. But before that? Before the first word spoken by God, what was there? It was from this silence that language was born. In wakening into life, and therefore to consciousness, man found himself enclosed in a silence that exceeded him and at the same time provoked him. He broke the silence in order to fulfill himself, in accordance with the divine will, and began, like God, to make use of language.
>
> Thence comes this tension in us—the first tension, created by desire and violation—between spoken words, human language, and silence, which lays claim to being the language of God. The secret of the one matches the mystery of the other. But language, like silence, is not without its dangers; the poet and the visionary both bear the burning seal of the words behind words.
>
> In childhood, searching for the truth of despair,

man aspires with all his being to silence—to the mystic silence that suggests the inaccessible, the forbidden, and the beyond. Masters teach him how to purify everyday language through the silence of sacrifice, in order to hasten the end of all times. Let all men be silent, or speak without lying, without demeaning their souls, and the Savior will be there.

And when he will be there, men will come from all over to salute him with long cries of joy and songs of happiness.

But the Messiah, in his melancholy, will remain silent.

At that hour of the morning, Brooklyn is in turmoil. The streets are full of people in a hurry. Old Hasidim, with ritual objects under their arms, are running to *shachris,* the morning service. Ageless grandmothers, with black scarves over their heads, are going to open their husbands' bakeries and grocery stores. Children are climbing into the yellow buses that take them to the *heder* or to the school for little girls. People are talking Yiddish with all the accents of Central Europe. Acquaintances call out to one another, exchange the morning's news. Trouble in the outside world? That doesn't concern them. In Brooklyn the focus is on life in Brooklyn. Who said what about which rabbi or against his court. Certainly, they talk about Israel too. The Satmarer Rebbe's followers are passionately opposed to it; others defend it ferociously. Fanatics shout. Violence is in the air. Insults, threats, oaths; it doesn't take much for them to come to blows. The fanatics invoke the Torah to justify their hatred of the other: They forget that whoever makes use of the sacred scrolls as instruments of murder is himself guilty of murder. And yet, there is also the general mood of study and prayer that somehow brings them all together.

For the Days of Awe are approaching; Rosh Hashanah and Yom Kippur, the days when the King of the Universe will judge the nations and cause men to tremble, are only a week away.

Elsewhere, in Manhattan and all over the planet, it is events of another kind that interest people. History, in the grip of upheavals, experiences highs and lows at a vertiginous pace. A wave of liberation has been sweeping across the continent of Europe. The dictatorship in Poland is finished. The bloody tyrants in Czechoslovakia and Romania have exited. The Berlin Wall has been demolished. Everywhere, joyful crowds celebrate the triumph of their democratic aspirations. Everywhere the chains are falling off. It seems that the last decade of the century offers a powerful message of happiness for generations to come.

But the forces of evil have not abdicated. The malevolent ghosts of hatred are resurgent with a fury and a boldness that are as astounding as they are nauseating: ethnic conflicts, religious riots, anti-Semitic incidents here, there, and everywhere. What is wrong with these morally degenerate people that they abuse their freedom, so recently won? Such questions are not posed in Brooklyn. In Brooklyn they are rather more concerned with the accounts that each one will have to render to God on the day of the New Year, on judgment day, Rosh Hashanah. Before this Judge there will be only one question to answer: How have you spent your days and nights, what have you done with your talent?

Razziel knew the answer: His own life had been wasted. Since Kali's death he had reflected on it bitterly and resentfully, but it was too late to start again; Kali had taken it with her into the grave. His life's book was written and finished; it was impossible to modify its substance.

"From the mother's womb to the bowels of the earth," Paritus used to say, "the journey is a short one and the same for us all." "But where is the Eternal in all this?" the Jewish mystic Gdalya ben Jacob had asked him. "Can it not have some sway over the length—if not the direction—this journey takes?" "God watches, that's all," Paritus was said to have replied. "But it's when he is not watching that things grow complicated and become interesting." Too interesting, thought Razziel. Could that be man's goal, to live an "interesting" life? For Paritus, the essential quality of action was not to dissipate itself but to inscribe itself in an immutable time. And was not this time the time of death?

Lord, look at me. Do you but see me? asked Razziel. Are you present with me in my solitude? Are you my shelter or am I yours? I have been deprived of everything and abandoned by all; you are all I have in the world. You, my judge, are my dispenser of justice, my secret. What have I done?

Across the river from Brooklyn, Manhattan soars toward blue heights that are close but unattainable. A symphony of smells and languages, a kaleidoscope of colors and dreamlike events, a focal point for the daily brutality of men and of the fates that befall them, a center of attraction for ambitions, passions, aspirations, and conspiracies. People become rich or poor there, famous or forgotten, politically powerful or socially crushed—all in the twinkling of an eye. A chance encounter is enough to save you or ruin you. A handshake may carry you up into the seventh heaven or plunge you down to the ninth circle of hell.

Since Kali's death, Razziel had never been back to Manhattan. Rather than live in the comfortable apartment his father-in-law had given him, he had preferred his modest furnished room close to the yeshiva. There he had the bare necessities. A bed, a table, a few shelves for his books, a bathroom, a kitchenette—that was enough for him. Luxury had never appealed to him; after his marriage he accepted it only grudgingly. Why did affluence make him feel guilty? Kali would tease him: "You may be born to suffer, but I'm not." Was it true? Then Kali would say, "Look at you. If you're not suffering you reproach yourself and you end up suffering even more."

She understood so much, Kali. It was that wisdom that had attracted him. More than her beauty? Certainly as much, but differently. Even if it created tensions between them, their passion for truth reinforced their bonds. Kali was against self-censorship. She rejected constraints. Being both stubborn and adaptable, she helped her husband in his refusal of creature comforts and complacency. For Razziel, Kali represented an intellectual rigor and a spiritual ambition without which his inner strivings could never have reached their goal. Sometimes he quoted Paritus to her: "What people who are alternately attracted by language and by silence don't understand is that there can be silence in talk and talk in silence. They don't understand that what is revealed keeps its own mystery." Kali's reaction was always the same: "Tell your friend Paritus to stop getting on my nerves." Was it Paritus who provoked the quarrels that sometimes seemed to come between them? Was she jealous of him?

It had certainly not spoiled the all-too-brief years of a perfect marriage. They were deeply in love. Bound to each other, body and soul, they functioned as one. Life, for them, held the most prodigious of adventures, the most dazzling of passions. They loved to discover it, laughing, roaming in Central Park, visiting exhibitions. Sometimes, they would pretend not to know one another. Then they had to invent a new way of making an approach: "Are you a New Yorker, miss? No? May I be of assistance to you? Would you allow me to show you the way to the Statue of Liberty?" And Kali would join in the game. "Excuse me, I don't know you. Who do you take me for?" When he insisted on "explaining" a Goya or a Velázquez painting to her at the Metropolitan Museum of Art, she proved to him with disarming aplomb that she knew more about painting than he did.

Then things began to go wrong. The angels in heaven must have been jealous. As the years went by, Razziel seemed increasingly preoccupied with his buried past and this made him forget how to live in the present. He grew angry with himself for not being able to share everything with his wife. He would have liked to talk to her about his parents but he knew nothing about them. And he was tormented by his longing to see Paritus. His last message—from a remote province in India—had reached him three or four years ago. Was he ill? Dead, maybe? He had promised to see Razziel again, to help him unearth the secret of his past. Why had he not kept his promise?

And then Kali became pregnant. His joy did not last long, for she fell ill. Gravely ill. Even more than a husband, he had longed to be a father. "Everything will be all right," he told his wife. "You'll see. You'll get well soon. We'll have a son who—" And Kali would correct him in a weak voice: "Or a daughter." Razziel kissed her brow. "If she's like you, I agree." But Kali's condition grew worse. Doctors' visits, various tests, nuclear medicine, all kinds of therapies: Though she was aware of the seriousness of her condition, she did not stop smiling, but from one day to the next her smile grew paler. Never leaving her bedside, Razziel neglected his duties at the yeshiva. He asked for and was granted the prayers of several masters. Children in the schools recited psalms for her. In his mind, Razziel begged Paritus to come to his aid: Kali must come through, must be strong enough to give birth. When her parents, crushed by worry, came to visit them it was he who offered words of comfort. They would repeat over and over: "Why not consult another doctor, a greater specialist? We'll sell everything, we'll give anything. . . ." But there was nothing to be done. Too weak to read, Kali liked Razziel to read to her: newspaper articles, poems and essays by all kinds of authors, ancient texts. She would doze as she listened. Yet when Razziel stopped she would surprise him with her comments. "I'm so proud of you," he would say to her, kissing her. He learned to give injections and was always there when Kali needed them.

"How much time do I have left?" Kali asked him one morning, as he lay beside her.

"Everything to do with time is in God's hands, not the

doctors'," Razziel replied in a murmur. "But the doctors are confident. And God tells you not to resign yourself but to hold on, to fight. You're not alone. Take strength from me, from your parents, our friends."

"They're afraid to tell you the truth," Kali replied softly.

She went into decline at an alarming rate. She stopped eating and slept all the time. When she opened her eyes and looked at Razziel, she seemed to be begging for death.

There was no need for explanations. As on their first day, they knew. They had crossed a threshold. Kali's life was at its end.

Razziel also knew he would never be a father. His line would end with him.

It was a Jewish American industrialist, Arieh Leib Friedman, who had brought Razziel to the United States. Associated with an ultraorthodox organization concerned with Jewish refugees from Eastern Europe, he had learned from Paritus of the young prisoner's plight. Making use of his connections in high places, he had succeeded in obtaining his release. Razziel arrived in New York, equipped with a political refugee's visa, as a "relative" of his protector. Out of gratitude, as much as to ease the formalities, Razziel had adopted his surname. Accepted into a yeshiva in Brooklyn, yet again thanks to a recommendation from Paritus, who seemed to know everybody, he spent fruitful years there studying the sacred texts and the endless commentaries on them: the Talmud and its laws. Later, after his ordination, he was initiated into the esoteric sciences. He wrote an essay on the concept of exile in Jewish thought. Why does the Torah begin with the second letter, *beth,* rather than the first, *aleph*? Because the latter was already in exile. Exile is the principal theme of human existence. Adam and Eve were exiled from paradise. Thereafter the whole universe, and its creator too, lived in exile. In mourning, the prisoner of his creation, the Shekinah, weeps and cries out in silence; she desires to go home, return to her first dwelling, to be united with the source. Woe unto him who heareth not her lamentations. . . .

Razziel could have obtained a pulpit, but he preferred to devote himself to teaching, especially because his beloved Kali had refused to become a rabbi's wife, a *rebbitsin.* Her brother, Binem, had been a student at the yeshiva. Invited by his father to come and celebrate the Sabbath with the family, Razziel had met Kali, a slim young woman with long brown hair, bubbling with wit and self-confidence. Even when she lost her temper, her angular face shone with her love of life. Some people thought of her as arrogant. That Friday evening at the dining table, she had become angry because her brother, who was both pious and timid, refused to talk about the obviously unscientific character of certain Bible stories. Though Razziel was immediately fascinated by the young woman, he made the mistake of coming to his pupil's defense. Kali took an instant dislike to him and let him feel it. Seeing him in sudden distress, her father consoled him. "Pay no attention to my daughter; she's only happy when she's making someone miserable. Tonight, it happens to be you."

The following week Razziel refused an invitation to spend the Sabbath with Binem's family again, and the third week too. The following Thursday it was Kali herself who arrived on his doorstep with a letter from her father. "I have a great favor to ask of you: Come and spend the Sabbath with us again. It will be a special one. It falls on an anniversary that has marked my life: that of my parents' arrival in America." And Kali added with a smile, "I promise not to tease you. Mind you, it won't be so much fun."

When she opened her lips she smiled. And when she smiled her eyes sparkled. Her father did not wait long to speak privately to Razziel: Why didn't he marry his daughter?

But Razziel was not ready for marriage. "I don't know if I have the right to start a family. First of all I must learn who I am and who my parents are. Even if they're dead, I have a duty to invite them to the wedding. Let us wait a little. Paritus will come to our aid. Kali will understand."

Kali's father sought the intervention of friends. Then he took Razziel to see Rebbe Tzvi-Hersh of Kamenets, the descendant of a celebrated Hasidic Master. The old man radiated kindness. Seated in his armchair, he welcomed Razziel with outstretched hands.

"I have heard a great deal about you, young man. What the Talmud says of Akiba ben Yoseph also applies to you: Your fame travels from one end of the world to the other. People speak to me in praise of your learning and your piety. But why do you wish to live alone? You should take a wife, build a house, assure the survival of our people—is that not the first commandment of the Torah?"

And without allowing his visitor to interrupt, he began enumerating the virtues of married life. You can serve God by making yourself useful to mankind; you can liberate the Messiah from his prison by consoling a being in distress; or you can celebrate divine law simply by bringing up a child in the faith of our ancestors.

Razziel listened to him with a heavy heart. Out of respect for the Rebbe, he chose not to show that his arguments had failed to convince him. But the old man guessed, for he invited him to come and spend the following Sabbath under his roof, so they could continue their conversation.

During the service and at mealtimes the Rebbe's followers sang and danced, praising the Lord for having made the Sabbath the object and soul of Creation. Razziel held back. He felt painfully like a stranger. Desolate, he wondered why he had been invited, since no one was paying any attention to him. But he was mistaken. During the third meal, while wistful regret was engulfing the Hasidim as the Sabbath drew to a close, someone joined him in his corner and asked him why he was not singing. It was G'dalia, a disconcerting young Hasid. Tall and emaciated, he exerted great influence on his fellow Hasidim: They called him "the dark one." The Rebbe loved him because he stood up to him. "The best proof that I'm not a rabbi," he would say, laughingly, "is that G'dalia is my Hasid."

G'dalia went up to Razziel and touched his arm. "You have blasphemed. Sadness is the negation of the Sabbath, which reflects the joy of the Creator as he contemplates his creation. Why did you refuse to sing?"

"I was not capable of it."

"You could have forced yourself."

"Isn't the use of force forbidden on the Sabbath?"

They had to break off their conversation. The third meal was coming to an end, they needed to attend *maariv,* evening prayers. The Rebbe withdrew, while his disciples gathered to start the week with study. At the other end of the room, old men were reminiscing: The great-grandfather of one of them had seen Rabbi Moshe Leib of Sassov dancing; the ancestor of another had been present when Rebbe Mendel of Kotsk, one Shabbat, had burst in on his followers and cried out with pain and rage. Terrified, they had all fled.

Razziel went out into the courtyard for some fresh air.

"Has the Rebbe upset you?"

G'dalia again. He was walking beside Razziel, who had not heard him approach.

"So, did he order you to get married?"

How did he know?

"It's a subject very close to his heart," G'dalia added. "Did you give him an answer?"

To his surprise, Razziel felt he could trust G'dalia and talk to him. He told him about Paritus. All through the night they walked up and down together. Thrusting his head forward, G'dalia wanted to know everything about this episode in Razziel's life. Now and then he interrupted him with a question or a remark, to clarify a particular detail. Thus, thanks to him, Razziel came to recall words and actions buried long ago in his subconscious.

When Razziel had nothing more to tell, he fell silent. For a long while G'dalia did nothing to break the silence, contenting himself with putting his arm around his new companion's shoulder, like an elder brother. After they had walked around the courtyard one more time, G'dalia said to him, "Don't wait for Paritus. Marry. But when he comes, let me know. I might have need of him myself."

But Paritus never came back.

Razziel finally allowed Kali to persuade him and the wedding took place. It was a magnificent affair: G'dalia accompanied the groom under the huppah; the Rebbe officiated at the ceremony and recited the seven blessings. Hasidic and other celebrities were present. Two masters preached the sermons for the occasion. Klezmer songs had been composed in the couple's honor. A postcard arrived from Paritus, mailed from Tashkent: *Achieving the goal does not signify the end of the quest.* For the first time there was harmony between body and soul. The young couple thrived. Kali was alternately joyous, tender, and full of mischief. She was passionate and curious, constantly questioning him about his life. Had he known women before? At what precise moment had his senses opened to desire? She wanted to know all about his parents, and his childhood, and found it hard to accept that this topic belonged in the zone of darkness that surrounded him. Then he talked to her about Paritus. She insisted that he reveal everything about him. Was it simple female jealousy on her part? She found her husband's attachment to this mysterious old character bizarre and sinister. Razziel came to believe that at the basis of all human truth there is a wounded consciousness, a bruised heart.

If only there were someone in the world who might one day continue my quest, mused Razziel, in great distress. Kali had so much hoped to have a child, and he even more so.

They had spoken of the child they so desperately longed for many times. He so wanted to be a father, because he had not been able to be a son. When Kali discovered she was pregnant they spent the whole night with their arms about each other. Then came that morning when the doctor shattered their hopes. Razziel held his wife's hand all night, but they did not exchange a single word. Soon after that she succumbed to the relentless disease.

Kali still smiled sometimes, but her smile was no longer the same. Before, when she smiled, earth and heaven united to sing of man's joy. But ever since her illness, she enveloped herself in silence. One day when Razziel played a record that she liked, she signaled for him to turn it off.

"Does it hurt you to listen?" Razziel asked her.

"No, I like listening." She choked back her tears and, struggling for composure, answered, "I prefer . . . listening to you."

He sang her melodies that reminded her of happy nights spent with the Hasidim.

"What becomes of life when it leaves us?" asked Kali. "Where does it go? Tell me, what will become of my life when I am no longer here to contain it?"

Razziel remembered a question Paritus had put to him: "What becomes of the sound the wind makes when it shakes the tree?"

"I don't know," Razziel had replied.

"That's because you don't know how to listen. Know, then, that the sound remains within the tree. It will never leave it."

Now Razziel paraphrased these words for Kali. "Your life will remain within me. It will never leave me."

"And I?"

"You as well. You will remain within me."

Then one night the eyes of the sick woman, who had already lost all memory, absorbed the darkness in which she was drowning.

IT WAS two o'clock in the morning, and the Judge had still not reappeared. The anxiety weighing more and more heavily on the prisoners was tangible. There is nothing worse than uncertainty. A mad thought, which Yoav quickly banished, flashed through his mind: Was it thus that his grandparents had found themselves in a little room, prisoners in the ghetto, and then in the railroad car whose skylights were closed off with barbed wire? Take care, he told himself. No comparisons. It's vital not to draw analogies. Tirelessly Bruce went on banging on the door, but no one responded. Claudia too lashed out in anger, but to no avail. They were not aware that the Hunchback was watching them and the total absence of reaction unnerved them. The Judge is waging psychological warfare on us, thought George. Is that part of his plan?

A month earlier, when consulting the archives relating to Abraham Lincoln and the Civil War, George had been surprised to discover a document written in German that clearly had been misfiled. It concerned a ghetto in Eastern Europe that had been liquidated in 1942. A Wehrmacht captain was giving an account to his divisional general of the logistical support he had provided for the Einsatzkommandos charged with the extermination of the Jews in the area. Although not a Jew himself, George had read the document with more than usual interest: Pamela was Jewish. Besides, the Holocaust had fascinated him for a long time. The fact that the killers thought it necessary to write everything down, to record it all on paper—in other words, to serve as bookkeepers and archivists—intrigued him above all else. Little by little he had read everything on the subject he could lay his hands on: histories, memoirs, and eyewitness accounts, as well as transcripts of the various trials of war criminals in Europe and in Israel. These studies had brought him closer to his Jewish colleagues and to Pamela's Jewish friends, and it was she who introduced him to a certain Boaz, an "archivist" in the Israeli secret service. Pamela was convinced that, at a certain period in his career, Boaz had taken part in operations designed to track down and arrest those primarily responsible for the "final solution" in occupied Poland. On the advice of the Department of Justice and with the agreement of the State Department, George had contacted his Israeli colleague and accepted his invitation to come and see him in Jerusalem. Boaz would certainly help him to discover more about the case that preoccupied him.

The document in question bore the signature of an Austrian politician, a current member of the government, known for his pro-Jewish and pro-Israeli views. If his past came to the surface, his political future would be called into question and perhaps irrevocably compromised. Now, sitting in this room, he considered what action to take. Destroy the document before it fell into the hands of the Judge, whose moral character was, to say the least, doubtful? Swallow it as spies do in the movies? Moved by a sudden inspiration, George decided to share his secret with Yoav. He took him into a corner and, very quietly, told him about his dilemma. The others, believing the two were discussing a plan of escape, spoke louder in order to cover up their whispering.

"Can a man expiate his crimes and repent?" asked George. "And become innocent in his own eyes?"

Yoav replied that, being neither a rabbi nor an expert in matters of ethics, he did not feel qualified to give him an opinion.

"I understand you," said George. "I think like you. I don't believe I have the right to judge. But I'm relying on my colleague, your fellow countryman, to help me. He must have a dossier on this Austrian officer. The Nuremberg Tribunal only sat in judgment on the Gestapo and the SS, not the Wehrmacht. Thus, my man must have slipped through the denazification process without too much difficulty. Did he try to redeem himself in some way or other? Has he repented? More to the point, is the influential minister of today the same man who assisted—and maybe took part in—the massacre of twelve hundred and forty Jews in the Kovno ghetto? "

As he spoke, George became more and more excited. Occasionally, he took out his handkerchief to mop his brow, moist with perspiration. He wanted the other man to understand what was at stake: It was a question not only of the honor of an individual but also of members of his family who were in no way responsible for his actions. And then there were the implications of the affair for the Austrian people on the one hand and the people of Israel on the other.

"Believe me," said George, betraying his distress, "I've never been in a situation like this before. I've always lived in a world of paper. My research could harm no one. Whereas now . . ."

Yoav did nothing to interrupt him. In his thoughts he was back in the room at Sloan-Kettering. A particularly attentive young German was among the group of doctors clustered around the senior oncologist considering his case. Sharp-nosed and with his blue-gray eyes hidden behind horn-rimmed spectacles, this doctor showed a particular interest in the young patient from a distant land, and they had had occasion to converse, especially in the evenings, when Carmela went back to her hotel and the sounds in the hallway became muffled.

During the first few weeks they discussed the situation in Israel, about which Dr. Heinrich Blaufeld, "for obvious reasons," as he put it, displayed great curiosity and indeed profound sympathy. Later, their conversations revolved chiefly around the terrible illness that was sapping the Israeli officer's body, thrusting him inexorably toward death.

"Why did you choose the military?" asked the doctor.

"Where I come from," replied Yoav, "it's not a question of choice but of necessity; we Jews in Israel plan to survive. Weak and defenseless, we would have no chance; recent history—ours and yours—is proof of this. Jewish weakness may arouse either scorn or pity, but not support and certainly not respect. So we had to look for something else. It's true that our military strength provokes envy, but we couldn't survive without it."

The doctor looked uneasy. "Do you hold it against me that I'm German?"

"No," said Yoav, after a moment's thought. "You're too young to be responsible for—"

"Suppose I were not so young?"

"You should thank heaven that you are."

"Heaven has nothing to do with it."

He left the room on the pretext of an urgent errand, but an hour later he returned, took a chair, and drew it up to the bed.

"I want to be truthful with you," he said. "I'm German, and I grew up in a family where love of the Fatherland was a sacred tradition, even when our country had been debased. Then one day I learned to my horror that my father—a doctor renowned as much for his skills as for his compassion—had served in the SS. Worse, he had taken part in the 'selections' at Birkenau. That day I was tempted to abandon my studies and travel as far away as possible. More precisely, I wanted to turn my back on everything, to become another person, to die. I'd had enough. And yet I lacked nothing. As the eldest son of a well-to-do family who moved in the highest social circles, there was nothing I couldn't have—in terms of what money can buy, at least. Becoming aware of my distraught state, my mother questioned me for days. I told her nothing; why upset her? Did she know her husband had committed crimes against humanity, the same humanity he was now trying to save?

"One night I decided to seek an explanation from my father. 'How could you?' I asked. He did not even defend himself. He simply said, 'Just as there are predatory birds, so there are predatory ideas: I came under their spell.' Then: 'Just as the survivors say that no one will ever understand the victims, what I must tell you is that you will never understand the executioners.' Then, changing his tone, he added a little sentence that still haunts me. 'I could have been judged then, but not now.' Well, our conversation made me even more unhappy. I thought, I want to understand; with all my heart I burn to understand. And I'm afraid that one day I shall no longer want to. I said this to my father, and he received it like a slap in the face."

Slumped on his chair, his face pale, the young doctor held his head in his hands and fell silent. Discreetly, Yoav looked away, lest he might catch him in tears.

"My father died shortly after that," continued the doctor. "And I continued my studies of medicine. I set myself the goal of making reparation for my father's crimes by specializing in extreme cases: I want to help those the world has turned its back on. You understand me, don't you?" Then, after a pause: "I would give everything to save your life, or at least to prolong it; you know that too, don't you?"

Yoav raised himself on his pillow. "Maybe Ivan Karamazov was right: I might possibly be able to forgive what has been done to me as a Jew, but not what was done to us as men." Then he went on. "No, I can't forgive anything. Do you know the writings of the great French philosopher, Vladimir Jankelevitch? He said there are cases where there should be no forgiveness. He was Jewish."

He held out his hand to the doctor, with a smile. "Just think, if I had not been ill we should never have met."

The doctor smiled back at him. "This time I really think providence may have had a hand in it."

The next day, Yoav told Carmela about their conversation. She exclaimed, "Well, if he can make you better, I'll forgive him anything he likes."

While he was listening to George, Yoav was asking himself, If that young doctor had been here tonight what would he have done? Would he have volunteered to be a scapegoat? In that case, why shouldn't I? My days are numbered, whatever happens. Dying to save human lives—isn't that a soldier's duty? It's true I'm not alone in the world. I have Carmela. Do I have the right to make such a decision without consulting her? How would she advise me?

He recalled the words of the German doctor at their last meeting. "Don't forget that the Jews were not the only victims of my father and his accomplices: we, their children, are victims too. In our own way, we too have been uprooted and left on the scrap heap. For the children of the executioners too, midnight will always be sounding. Don't forget that."

"I won't forget," Yoav had said. He had not expected to be so deeply touched.

"I know," said the German doctor. "You are Jewish, and the Jews forget nothing. But being a Jew, you also ought to believe in miracles. That is important for a sick man like you. Faith is as important as the most powerful of drugs."

Yoav had a sudden vision of his father, who had believed in miracles. "But do I?" he asked himself.

Miracles were for other people. It's always other people who need them. They happen for all kinds of people but not me. I have to get by without them. The prisoner cannot free himself from his own prison, says the Talmud. Nor can the sick man heal himself. But what about God, Father? God has need of man in order to be God. Who knows? Perhaps he too needs miracles.

The Judge returned just before three o'clock in the morning. He looked preoccupied as he sat down amid icy silence. His eyes fixed on the ceiling, he began ruminating on guilt and death.

"What is innocence? Personally, I don't believe in it. What is it, other than an excuse for imbeciles and a matter of luck for the lucky and the fools? For them, as for the rest of us, it's the tip of the iceberg that rises above the mountain of sins and crimes committed in its name that we all carry around with us. And what is life? A tiny wretched island amid the infinite and majestic ocean of death."

The survivors did not dare look at one another. Was he still making fun of them? Why did he choose this night to hold forth on metaphysical questions as old as humanity? Was it a new game? The guy's crazy. What lunatic asylum has he escaped from? What bar has he stumbled out of? Either he's been drinking or else he's just plain nuts. But he went on rambling in a monotonous drone that in other circumstances would have put his listeners to sleep. He quoted from Plato and Seneca, Nietzsche and Augustine, Gypsy legends and the Tibetan Book of the Dead. As he became more and more excited, his arguments grew confused and he completely lost the thread of his harangue. Eventually, he calmed down, stared fixedly at his five prisoners, and continued in solemn tones.

"True innocence is not life but death. The death of one person absolves the others. So that some men may live, another man must die. This is what I have learned from my Masters, who repeat it to me every month in my dreams, so as to afford you—or people like you—salvation. Listen to them. Listen to me. To wash away his guilt, man must submit and enter into death. And Death, graciously and peacefully, welcomes him with open arms. But in return Death must be welcomed in the same manner. Are you ready to assume your innocence?"

Did he expect a reply, a commitment? Applause, perhaps? As they all remained silent, he shook his head in disgust and went out, leaving behind him an acrid smell that none of his victims could identify.

The door opened noiselessly and the Hunchback appeared, his customary teapot in his hand.

"Who's cold? Who's thirsty? The tea's hot, the coffee's strong. I'm here to serve you."

They bombarded him with questions that he left unanswered. Inexplicably, their attitude toward him had changed. They smiled at him, they promised him gifts, they tried to win him over: Was he not the messenger, the representative of the gods, of the other side? Grimacing politely, he listened to what they said to him, heard their promises, but affected to be deaf. Nevertheless, being human after all, he cast timid glances in Claudia's direction. Did he think she was smiling at him? He made her a gift of his most beautiful thought.

And suddenly, as he was filling their cups, as if it had been his function from birth, from the beginning of the world, he waxed eloquent.

"Drink up, drink up, my friends, it will do you a world of good. I've made this tea myself, and the coffee too. I'm your friend, you must believe me. I wish you no harm; I wish no one to harm you. The Judge is deliberating with his superiors. That's all part of the game—if it is a game. . . .

"Don't ask me who his superiors are. I don't even know if they exist. But *he* exists, there's the rub. What has made him cruel? When did he encounter evil? How did he come to espouse it? What tragedy has he lived through that has made him so bitter? I think he married young, but that's not certain. Nothing's certain where he's concerned.

"He's told me a great many things about a great many people in a way that made me think he was talking about himself. Was his mother a whore? Was his father a saint? Why should he tell me so? Did his wife and his daughters really die in a fire? With the proceeds from the insurance, he began to gamble. He hasn't stopped since. And, see here, even about this I'm not absolutely sure. You never know with him. Anyone, apart from me, can make him change his mind at any moment for no apparent reason. It's happened to him lots of times. Believe me, I could tell you some stories. . . . Only last week he sent me to the pharmacy to bring him some very strong sleeping pills. 'But what about the prescription?' I said to him. 'The pharmacist knows me,' he replies. 'Tell him to call me.' So I put my boots on and walk through the snow. I get out of breath, stumble and fall down, I pick myself up, I curse him for ever having taken an interest in me, and there I am in front of the pharmacy. As always, my poor heart is thumping twice as fast as usual. Am I going to see the pharmacist's wife again? No luck; it's her husband who serves me. I tell him why I've come, and he says to me, 'I see. So your boss has no desire to live anymore.' But when I got back I found out: Those sleeping pills, he didn't want them for himself; he didn't need them. He wanted them for me! Can you imagine? For me—and I sleep even when I'm not asleep. He wanted to make me take them! As I can't refuse him anything, I was about to obey him. I already had a glass of water in my hand. Then at the last minute he informs me that his masters have set aside the sentence.

"What can you do? That's how he is, the Judge. So? If I were you I would be careful. First of all, if he gives you drugs, refuse them. Second, don't rule out the possibility that, with you, his game isn't a game at all."

Was the Hunchback worried about Claudia, thanks to whom he had suddenly felt capable of love? Of course, he knew that she could never love him. He had no illusions. But in his mind, if someone loved a person, it was as if he loved the whole world. And to love is also to inspire love, to make yourself loved.

"For somebody here," he said, more softly, "tonight is the first night of his life. Don't ask me who it is. But for somebody else, if the Judge is to be believed, tonight is the last. Once again, don't ask me who it is. I don't know myself. All I know is that I want to be your friend."

Surreptitiously glancing at the woman, so beautiful and so close, he left the room with a sigh.

For whatever reasons, the survivors took the Hunchback's words seriously. In effect the Judge was forcing each of them to respond to the question, at once so simple and so complex: Why do you want to live?

"Let's do something, anything," said Claudia frantically. "Doing nothing drives me crazy. Look, the Judge wants to sit in judgment. So let's make believe we're in court. What do we have to lose?"

"But we've been doing nothing else all night," Bruce protested.

"We need to go further."

And Claudia explained. To respect the rules of the game, they needed to act as if it were not a game. They all needed to take it seriously and go along with the Judge. In other words, each of them had to consider his or her death to be close at hand. "Since we're all in the same boat, each one of us should cite the most important reasons why he or she should be spared."

Why not? thought Razziel. After all, isn't it incumbent on us to justify every hour, every moment of our lives?

"Since it's your idea," said Bruce, still hostile, "I suggest you start."

"I love a man," said Claudia.

Bruce burst out laughing. "Bravo! Congratulations!"

Claudia had tears in her eyes, she felt vulnerable, something that did not often happen to her. "His name is David."

"You're in love with David, fine. And you believe this gives you the right to live, is that right?"

"It's very recent," said Claudia, embarrassed and unhappy. "We haven't had time to experience our love to the fullest. We've only lived its first few moments."

She fell silent, regretting that she had confided in the others. To regain her composure she started to bring out her lipstick but resisted the impulse. David hated seeing her wearing makeup.

George, too, could have spoken of his love—for Pamela—but he said, "I have a mission to carry out. It's of the highest importance, I assure you."

"A mission? What kind of mission?" asked Bruce.

"I'm not at liberty to tell you."

Bruce made a face. "In that case, it doesn't count."

George pointed to Yoav. "Ask the officer. He knows."

"It's true. I know what it's about," said Yoav.

"So does that give him more of a right to be spared than the rest of us?"

"I didn't say that. That's not up to me or you to decide. You're eager enough to stay alive yourself, if I'm not mistaken. Tell us, Mr. Schwarz, what entitles you to special consideration?"

"I have an injustice to make right," Bruce admitted, ill at ease. "It's an injustice no one else can redress."

Next all eyes focused on Razziel.

"And your reason for wanting to preserve your life tonight?" He could have answered, I have loved, yes, I have loved a woman. Her name was Kali. She is dead. Is that a good reason for wanting to live? Instead he said, with a little cough, "I must meet somebody."

"Somebody. That's a bit vague," parried Bruce. "Is it a relative? A client who owes you money? An enemy you want to destroy?"

Razziel was at a loss. How could he describe Paritus? How could he define him? How could anyone measure objectively the importance of their meetings? The last time they had seen each other the old mystic had given him his blessing: "Keep your fervor, even in suffering." He had said "fervor," not "faith." And then he had added, "One day I'll tell you about the prophet, the artist, and the madman. Do you remember? In prison I said a few words about them to you, but not enough; the time was not ripe." Razziel had not understood: Who was he talking about? But he was used to not understanding his old friend. How would Paritus have advised him to answer Bruce? That every life is of divine essence? That the life of the prophet is worth exactly the same as that of the madman? That the very mystery of existence is what makes it unique and irreplaceable?

"You wouldn't understand," he said with a shrug.

"That's your problem," was Bruce's comment.

Yoav was the last to have to defend his right to life. Should he tell them he was ready to sacrifice it? He remembered a story his mother told him. He was five years old. Injured in a car accident, he was taken to the hospital. While they were operating on him, his father prayed and offered God a bargain: "If you need a life, take mine." On whose behalf would he, Yoav, offer God a similar bargain? Carmela's, certainly. His mother's, naturally. But the people in this room, what did he owe them? What did he know of their lives and why they wanted to save them? Even if he said, Fine, I'll die for you, they would want to know why. And he did not want their pity.

"I'm just like you," he said finally. "I have the same rights as you. But I have an idea: Suppose we draw lots?"

The suggestion, though logical, seemed to frighten them. To agree would mean to admit that a line had been crossed and that they were close to the inevitable outcome.

They withdrew into themselves to give free range to ghosts held prisoner by the past.

For Bruce, life was nothing but a game. Sometimes you win, sometimes you lose. What matters is to be ready to start playing again the next morning. That's what he had done all his life.

At school he used to amuse himself by being friendly to his classmates one day and contemptuous the next. To his parents he showed anger: "You want me to be a good student; that's your problem, not mine. I learn, I go on learning—what for? I can never learn everything. First, life will prevent me from doing that and then death will." As a teenager he continually challenged his father's authority; later, the rules of society. The game that fascinated him the most? Love; not his own but other people's. In fact, the concept of love was so intolerable to him that he invented a thousand tricks to corrupt it by the very act of laying claim to it.

He did not look like a Don Juan, precisely because he

tried too hard. He was built like a boxer, with a flattened nose and bushy hair. He had an aura of brute physical strength that should have kept women away rather than attracting them. The strange thing was that only women already in love, married or engaged, were attracted to him. His intuition helped him seek them out. He recognized them from their way of walking, dreaming, listening. Sometimes he addressed women in the guise of a disinterested friend, or a psychologist, or else a novelist in search of subject matter—in other words, a confidant—to whom everything can be confessed without fear. He got them to talk about their studies, their favorite pastimes, their fiancés, their problems. He took them to the theater, gave them birthday presents, and did his best to entertain them, persuading them that he was doing all this to enrich their lives. It amused him but he himself had no stable relationship.

He had succeeded in breaking off innumerable engagements, causing countless young people to shed countless tears.

The first time it was his tailor's daughter. They went to the same high school. A quiet, gifted, beautiful girl, Laura had fallen for Johnny, the dunce of the class. If she but looked at Johnny he felt less of a fool. Jealous of their friendship, Bruce decided to destroy it. He sent the girl flowers, love letters, and pleaded with her not to commit "the greatest folly" of her life.

This first attempt at diverting love was crowned with success; now Laura only had eyes for Bruce. She broke with Johnny, who became ill and never returned to school. A few weeks later Bruce abandoned her. She was devastated.

To his parents, who decried his boorish conduct, Bruce replied with a shrug, "The stupid girl didn't understand it was only a game." When his parents finally understood, it was too late.

Similar games followed. There was an unmarried woman who had finally found a suitor. A widow who was planning to remarry. The only daughter of an elderly mathematics teacher. A Spanish dancer who divorced her husband in order to follow him, only to return, devastated, to her own country when he abandoned her.

The teacher's daughter took her own life. After a week of mourning, her father came knocking at the door of the man he knew to be the cause of his misfortune.

"Look at me," he said. "You have killed my only daughter and, through her, other human beings yet to be born. She would have married and had children I was ready to love. Did you know that my entire family died in the turmoil in Europe? By killing my daughter, by stealing her love, you have destroyed my hopes. You didn't even love her. Tell me, why did you do it?"

There was no trace of anger in his voice, no hatred in his eyes. Only a terrible sadness, mingled with resignation.

Bruce was about to launch into his usual refrain, that it was only a game, a game whose cruel consequences were not his fault, but faced with this father in mourning, bowed by loneliness and grief, he could not open his mouth; the words turned to ashes in his throat. If only he could say something, do something, to banish the grief that confronted him. If only the earth, which he felt giving way beneath his feet, could swallow him up. That was the moment he faced the abyss and knew that he had to retrace his steps.

Now Bruce was on the way to Israel to find Stacy, his would-be latest victim—and his love. He had met her at a students' reunion. He had liked her joie de vivre. They spent several nights together in the Arizona desert before going on to New York. Then she left him to spend several weeks in a religious kibbutz in Galilee.

She had the right to know the truth, the whole truth. He would confess to her as he had never confessed before. He would show her that he was wearing the red scarf she had given him. He would ask her to marry him. And she would say yes.

David, thought Claudia. David, my love. David who has taught me to love love, with no regrets or compromise.

David's voice. David's lips. The trembling of his body at the moment when desire meets desire, when the heart is stronger than reason.

Had it not been for David I would have lived a whole life, a thousand lives, and never tasted love. Never known the sadness and the joy of passion. I would have lived out my life, a life of solitary death, as a neutral and indifferent spectator. Thank you, David, my love. Thank you for having shown me, thank you for having allowed me to show you that one shared night can transcend its limits and become an eternity.

Claudia had just left the theater. She was unhappy with the rehearsals. The play was dismal, lacking in fire; the language was trite; the actors' performance poor. How was she going to sell this disaster to the critics and then to the public? She had stopped at her office to pick up her coat when her private phone started ringing. Who could that be, she wondered. She ran over in her mind the people who knew her unlisted number. Her ex-husband, who could not fall asleep? A former lover whom she no longer cared for? A newspaper publisher who doted on her? She answered the phone.

"Yes?"

"Claudia?" said a man's voice.

"Who is this?"

"David."

She quickly checked through her mental file. She knew no one of that name.

"A mutual friend asked me to contact you."

"Who's that?"

"I'll tell you after . . ."

"After what?"

"After the dessert, before the coffee."

"What if I say no?"

"You'll get no dessert."

She looked at her watch. It was still early, and she had a free evening. Why not? An hour or two with a stranger is better than a night alone.

"Come and pick me up here," she said, sounding directorial. "I hope you're not far away: I hate to be kept waiting."

She did not have to wait long. David had called from a hotel near the theater. She had hardly repaired her makeup before he appeared in the doorway of her office.

What was Claudia's first impression? She was not bowled over: not tall enough, not young enough, not macho enough, not elegant enough. In fact, you wouldn't give him a second glance.

What an idiot I am, Claudia said to herself. This time I've really goofed. But when, as in a fairy tale, he took her arm and said to her, "A truly feminine face needs no makeup," Claudia blushed. She was about to reply, but he didn't give her the chance. "And that's true of life, too." He squeezed Claudia's arm more firmly. "Let's go for a walk."

All at once, nothing was as before. There was something in the way he held her arm and in his voice that touched the loneliness deep inside her. She felt she existed "differently" for someone who, unwittingly, had already become a part of her inner landscape. Appearances can be deceptive. What she was discovering at that moment in the man at her side was a secret beauty, an unsuspected grace, an originality, and a charm to which no one else, she was certain, could be receptive: God had created them for her alone.

They walked slowly, silently, through the little streets around New York University.

"Let's just look," said David. "This is our world."

"There are people fighting to change it."

"So what? They're a part of it too."

Students and tourists took notice of one another with the same interest or the same indifference. Street vendors were selling ties, carpets, watches, leather purses. Occasionally, drug dealers passed little packets with disconcerting rapidity to passersby pretending to be there by pure chance. David and Claudia went to a noisy little Italian restaurant. Claudia was about to remark that she loathed noise, but then changed her mind; the noise had subsided. Her body was speaking to her louder than the giant city. All she could hear was the pulsing of her own heart. She had not known that her body possessed so many voices.

"Are you hungry?" asked David, slipping his arm around her waist.

Claudia, though not accustomed to such familiarity, took it in stride.

"No," she said. "How about you?"

"Me, I'm hungry."

"OK, then I am too."

A vegetarian, he ordered pasta and green salad for the two of them. And white wine. And a fruit salad.

"You see. No one can say I deprived you of dessert."

She smiled.

"OK, now you can ask me any question you like."

"Let's start with the simplest. Which of my friends asked you to call me?"

"I can't recall."

"I don't believe you."

"He asked me not to recall."

"Don't you care that I don't believe you?"

"No problem."

"About everything or just that question?"

"About everything. But . . ."

"But . . . ?"

"I want you to trust me. And that's *not* the same thing."

She smiled at him again and thought, If he goes on looking at me like that, I don't have a chance.

"OK. It's not the same thing."

He seized her hand and held it under the table.

"Next question?"

"Who are you?"

"Don't be so nosy, young lady."

"I want to know. If you'll tell me I'll give you a kiss."

"Fine. But first I shall have to pry apart the jaws of time."

Spoken by someone else, this heavy phrase might have shocked Claudia. But it did not.

"Right," she said. "What are you waiting for? Pry away."

"I'm doing it."

"For yourself or for me?"

"For anyone who has to throw off the constraints of time, ego, and imagination."

"Are you good at imagining things?"

"Yes."

"In that case, imagine I've just given you a kiss."

She had thought that would make him laugh.

"I've just taken delivery of it," he said gravely.

"Whereabouts?"

"On my lips and in my heart."

Be careful, a voice within warned her; he's talking like someone onstage. Just listen to him, listen to yourself: You sound like characters in a play. But she silenced the voice. That's enough. I've spent my whole life being careful. Was that why all her relationships had been short-lived? Why her marriage had failed? She had checked her impulses, never completely let go, as if some uncontrollable force were always holding her back. But now that was all over. Understood?

The waiter brought them their coffee.

"I work at a theater," said Claudia. "What do you do?"

"I keep quiet."
"That's not a profession."
"You didn't ask me my profession, you asked what I do."
Taken aback, Claudia had an impulse to kiss him.
"But when you're not keeping quiet, what do you do?"
"A whole heap of things," he replied evasively.
"A heap, how many's that? Ten? Twenty-six?"
"I write."
"You're a writer?"
"I didn't say that. I said I write."
"What do you write?"
"Haven't I told you already? A whole heap of things."
"Novels?"
"Yes. Novels."
"Poems?"
"Poems, too."
"May I read them?"
"Sure."
"Where are they?"
"In my head."
She burst out laughing. "You're funny!"
"Sometimes what I write is funny."
"And other times?"
"Sad."
"Sad, you?"
"Yes. No. Sometimes what I write is sad."
"Even when you're happy?"
"Even when I'm happy."
"I'd like to read what you write. Now."
He did not reply.

They left the restaurant, went back to his hotel, and, once the door had closed behind them, gently, very gently, without the slightest haste, embraced.

And for each the other's body became a refuge.

The next day David took a plane back to Tel Aviv.

ABRUPTLY, at about four o'clock in the morning, the lights went out.

At first, they thought it was a power failure that would be quickly repaired, but it continued and the darkness finally became oppressive. Bruce took out a box of matches and Claudia her lighter, an army lighter David had given her. They lit up at the same time. The room seemed to shrink. Yoav was standing at the window, looking out. The snow, shimmering with a milky glow, was still falling with a constant rhythm, ready to absorb the dirt of roads, of trees, and even people.

"The bastard," said Bruce, "he's pushing us to the wall."

He thumped on the table. Nothing. George knocked on the door.

"Louder!" shouted Claudia.

Still nothing. The tension between the hostages was becoming palpable, and their nerves were beginning to fray. By now they were convinced that real danger lay in wait for them. The Judge represented an occult and malevolent power; he had them in his clutches, like toys. Was he going to permit a murder—or even commit one—in obedience to the voices of his Masters?

Squabbles broke out among them in the darkness, futile, almost incongruous, but tainted with infectious and absurd hostility. Well, here we are, Claudia said to herself, right in the middle of Sartre's *No Exit*. We hardly know one another, but very soon we're going to be bound by fear and hatred.

She was right. Each of them resented the others' presence as an unbearable intrusion. "Give me room to breathe!" "Will you stop stepping on my toes!" One reproached himself for having taken that ill-starred flight, the other for having accepted shelter in this accursed house. The third blamed the rest of the group for the whole situation and resented them for not having the courage or magnanimity to volunteer for death. They all had particular reasons for claiming favorable treatment, mercy for themselves. All save Yoav. He asked for nothing and clung to nothing.

The Judge's prolonged absence only increased the tension. What was he going to think up next? What was the import of his obscure speeches? What satanic cult held him in thrall?

Bruce was the first to lose what was left of his cool. Swinging his abominable red scarf around his head as if it were a weapon, he began to yell obscenities and wild threats. "I'm going to kill them, I tell you, I'm going to kill these monsters. Rip out their eyes, their ears, and their guts! I'll teach them to attack innocent people. That goddamned judge should be strung up, for real, and the Hunchback flogged till he begs for mercy!" No one dared to shut him up; in moments like this it was better to let rage spill out in great waves. He would end up exhausting himself. But he was beyond exhaustion. "That bastard of a judge, that son of a bitch, he'll pay for this. And that travesty of humanity, that mincing hunchback, he's got it coming." Razziel, too, was panic-stricken and began singing a song he had learned from the Rebbe of Kamenets: "You are my Lord and I am thankful to you." At the Rebbe's house, the Hasidim used to sing it loud and clear. Here, Razziel only hummed it softly.

But where had the Hunchback disappeared?

From time to time they all went "ssh," thinking they could hear the sound of voices coming from the corridor or from upstairs. Or were they mistaken? Their own silence hung in the silence that surrounded them.

The lights came on just as the Hunchback appeared in the doorway. He had a message from the Judge. "Tonight you will all be the judges. Whichever one of you is condemned, the survivors will all be responsible for that death. The person who is to carry out the sentence has already been appointed." He paused for breath, then: "That's all the Judge has instructed me to announce to you on his behalf. I wish I could tell you more, but that's all I know." And he left the room.

Through the window the snow could be seen, increasingly dense and turbulent, still falling inexorably, as if there were nothing amiss, as if five people were not in danger. In the village, people were eating, sleeping, and making love, while here five trapped human beings were desperately straining their ears to hear the approaching footfalls of death.

"Bastard, son of a bitch," yelled Bruce, like a gangster

double-crossed. "I'll kill him! I'll kill him with my bare hands! I'll tear him limb from limb and feed him to the wolves—no, to the jackals; wolves are too good for him."

"He's trying to set us against one another," said Razziel. "He mustn't succeed. We mustn't play his game."

But like it or not, they had to get involved.

Except, perhaps, for Yoav.

One hour before dawn, something happened that provoked a brief argument among the prisoners. The Hunchback came in to announce that the Judge wished to see Razziel outside. Outside in the cold? No: in his office. "What for?" Claudia asked. "Why does he want to see him? Why him rather than someone else?" Yoav suggested that he refuse in the name of solidarity: Together they would have a better chance of escaping. George asked the Hunchback's advice, who replied, "The Judge knows how to make himself obeyed." Razziel wondered what Paritus would have advised him to do. Doubtless not to shun the moment that may bring one closer to the truth. Isn't it incumbent on man to try to learn everything about his destiny at the very moment when he teeters on the brink of the void?

"You must come with me," said the Hunchback.

Razziel followed him into the corridor and from there into a little office, dimly lit but pleasantly heated. The walls were hung with portraits and old maps. Books were stacked in a corner; the Judge, on his knees, was rummaging through a pile of them.

"Sit anywhere you like," he said, without looking up.

Razziel sat on one of the two chairs. On a low table was a teapot, little cakes, dried fruit.

"Help yourself."

"I'm not hungry," replied Razziel.

The Judge seemed preoccupied as he leafed through a volume looking for some reference or forgotten statute. When he stood up, he took his place facing Razziel.

"So, you are well versed in mysticism."

Razziel remained silent.

"These matters interest me too."

Was he hoping Razziel would react? If so, it was a vain hope.

"What is it you seek in them? The mystery of the beginning or of the end?" The Judge's voice had changed. No longer threatening, it expressed true curiosity. "Is it a taste for the absolute that attracts you? For me it is initiation into death."

"Death is by definition absolute," Razziel said finally.

"Not at all. It's far too intermingled with life, which is anything but absolute. For me, the absolute lies in evil: pure evil, powerful, more powerful than goodness, and just as infinite as God. It is from evil that salvation will come."

Razziel shivered. Suddenly he understood the meaning of what was happening to him. In order to meet Paritus he first had to confront his adversary. Conversely, it was in order to discover this adversary that his meeting with Paritus had been ordained. Now he must be strong, he told himself, strong and lucid. He must be capable of saying the most obscure things in even tones, devoid of all emotion. There are certain words and silences that are worth more than all our emotions. Emotion only helps man to appease his conscience, to exonerate himself, to persuade himself that he is not as corrupt as all that, not as guilty as all that, since he suffers from the same wants as everyone else.

"Do you believe in Redemption?" asked Razziel in a hoarse voice.

"Which one?"

"There is only one," said Razziel. "The Redemption is the same in the present and in all eternity."

"And you, do *you* believe in it?"

"Yes. Every time a human being stops suffering and causes others to overcome suffering, he is experiencing the effect of Redemption. Saving the life of a child, rescuing a prisoner from torture, is to take part in the ultimate process that is Redemption."

The Judge shook his head. "If that is your great mystical quest, I find it pitiful, and you too. It is suited only to weak and sanctimonious souls, to pusillanimous ambitions. It rejects the violence of hatred or, at least, of anger; it lacks strength; and therefore it lacks humanity. Am I wrong?"

"Yes!" cried Razziel. "Rejecting violence and hatred demands more strength and more courage than yielding to them! Killing is easy; any fool or degenerate can do it. But giving meaning to life is a complex challenge of a quite different order."

"You accord too much value to life. Absolute good is meaningless, for it refers you back to God and his judgment. And that brings us back to our first question. For me, life is a curse. And there is evil in curses. In granting life, God simply reveals his own weakness. Do I shock you, sir, you, the specialist in esoteric matters? Have you not yet found in your texts the priceless evidence that proves the world can be saved by evil? Countless great minds have striven to arrive at this, by preaching goodness; they have all failed. That is why my Master has led me along the opposite road: We strive to save the world through evil. If you wish to know who was my Master I will tell you: He was an arsonist, a murderer."

The Judge fell silent. Razziel closed his eyes and again had a vision of Paritus. Ancient texts, inscribed on blazing parchments, came into his mind, the exploits of false messiahs and their disastrous consequences: Sabbatai Zevi in Turkey, Jacob Frank in Poland. They too believed they could change the course of History by violating its laws. And then there were the tragic lives of those pious dreamers, intoxicated with the absolute, who tried to force the Lord's hand by deepening their love for him and his creatures: Rabbi Abraham Abulafia and Rabbi Yoseph di la Reina. True mystery is not linked to messianic time but to the longing of man.

One day Paritus had asked him if he knew how to dance. No, he did not. "No?" Paritus was astonished. "You must learn. When you dance you lift yourself into the air. Only to fall back again? So what? When he comes back to earth, man is no longer the same." Once again, Paritus was right. Man's strength resides in his capacity and desire to elevate himself, so as to attain the good. To travel step by step toward the heights. And that is all he can do. To reach heaven and remain there is beyond his powers: Even Moses had to return to earth. Is it the same for evil?

Bizarrely, beyond the furious storm that buffeted the

walls as if to blow them away, the distant world seemed at peace, in full equilibrium. Time was becoming a thing one studied and questioned in order to calm it.

"Evil," said the Judge, "is what I know, as it knows me. It is all I know."

Razziel was preparing for a heartbreaking story: cruel parents, friendships betrayed, unhappy love. Maybe the Judge had grown up in prison, or on the streets. But no. He listened to a barely coherent account of a golden childhood; a youth full of promise, affectionate parents, inspired teachers. Then one day the teenager made the acquaintance of a strange guru with disconcerting ways and mesmerizing powers of denigration. He could read other people's thoughts and even control them. After this encounter, his life became a labyrinth, a laboratory where evil made all transmutations possible. Isn't evil, like suffering, the very essence of progress? the guru would ask. Isn't it necessary both for the functioning of justice and for the labors of theologians? There is no perfection except in evil, he often repeated. To do good is easy; it is the first rule they teach children. To do evil is not. Only a courageous spirit, burning with energy, is capable of rebelling against a thousand years of laws, social contracts, and religious dogmas.

Distancing himself little by little from his parents and their friends, the Judge began to follow the teaching of his guru. One day he saw a young handicapped boy fall on the pavement and went to help him up. The boy slipped and fell again. This time, as if happy to repair a foolish blunder, the Judge burst out laughing and turned away. On another occasion, he passed an old man in the street and knocked him over. Some years later, noticing a woman about to throw herself under a subway train, he held her back. By way of recompense she slapped his face. This experience marked a turning point in his life: He realized that seeing other people suffer made him happy. He adopted the custom of spending long hours in hospitals and prisons. The angels of evil had become his companions.

Suddenly the Judge stood up, lowered his head, took several steps across the room, and began speaking in a hoarse, bitter voice.

"To do evil and to serve evil is to recognize its timeless value. Have you ever seen the swollen face of a dead child, or the horrified expression of a young girl betrayed, or the torn bloody body of a violated mother? No? Then you will never know the attraction evil can hold for a man, to the point of making him an avenger, thirsty for justice. Such a man has only one desire, one ambition: to become a god of death by taking on its powers. Truth no longer lies in life but in death. It is in death that justice is accomplished. Killing the guilty man, eliminating the criminal: These things are no longer enough for him. He wants something more, something different. It is other people's innocence that he longs to strike down, because that of his own nearest and dearest has been soiled, disfigured, destroyed. He knows, yes, this man knows, that good has less power than evil and fewer possibilities. He does not know why God decided it thus, but let his will be done. And so he allies himself with evil, to sing its praise and become its messenger among those men who evidently need it in order to function." He lowered his voice. "You understand me, don't you? The mystic in you does understand me?"

"I understand that evil has its own priests as good has its

prophets. But I cannot accept that any man could wish to embody evil."

"Then you understand nothing!" exclaimed the Judge, suddenly radiant.

"What you say is immoral and inhuman," replied Razziel.

"What is inhuman, deriving pleasure from someone else's pain?"

"Yes."

"But that is where you're mistaken. For man, who cannot escape his condition, everything is human."

Razziel protested no further. Perhaps the Judge was right on that point. Man can both understand and cease to understand, love and despise, grasp existence at the moment that either imprisons or liberates him, experience the abyss even while his eyes are fixed on the heavens—and still be a man: that is, weak enough to be constantly changing his opinions.

"I may often be wrong," said Razziel, "but not about the fact that evil is the rejection and the negation of good and thus the rejection of life and of that which elevates man and allows him to transcend himself."

"And death? What do you make of death? Can one not transcend oneself in death?"

"No. Neither in mine nor in that of another. Death only means one thing: the end. The end of the world I carry within me. Beyond it, nothing in that world exists."

"But there is something else," said the Judge.

"Something else," echoed Razziel. "But that something else is beyond me and no longer depends on me. Or on you."

The Judge thought for a moment. "Do you know Cervantes had a very high opinion of Don Quixote? He said of him that what assured his success was dying a wise man, having lived as a madman. But it is also true that he strove to live above good and evil. How about you?"

At a sign of the Judge's, the door opened and Razziel rejoined his companions, wondering whether in fact the Judge had avenged the death of his wife and daughter.

Yoav listened to Razziel's report with half an ear; the existential conflict that arose between good and evil no longer concerned him. Yoav was thinking of his father. What would he have done in my place, he wondered, being a man for whom action was a kind of secular religion? In his youth in eastern Poland he had belonged to the clandestine Communist Party. Robust, with an ascetic face and an intense gaze, he was the very model of the romantic revolutionary who believes in the mystique of self-sacrifice in order to change the world. Inside him there was anger barely held in check, a rage just waiting for a pretext in order to explode. Later, in Israel, he became an officer in the commandos, but he rarely talked about his military activities.

One day, returning from an operation to intercept saboteurs in Galilee, he seemed devastated. "They killed two boys," he told Yoav. "We got there too late, three minutes too late. Yes, those bastards paid for it. But the boys, teenagers from a nearby kibbutz, I saw their mutilated bodies." He spoke in a barely audible voice, moving his hands nervously, obviously aching to do something useful, positive. "At times like this," he added hoarsely, "we're forever coming out with platitudes, like, Those two boys were heroes; they did not die in vain. And maybe in this case it's true, because our anger will survive them. And yet only fanatics—in religion as well as in politics—can find a meaning in someone else's death. That's what distinguishes them from mystics, or most of us, whose only concern is with our own death."

Standing at the window that looked out over their little garden, Yoav had listened to him intently, not knowing what to say.

"Come and sit by me," his father said.

They were alone in the house.

"I loathe violence," his father continued. "It's been repugnant to me ever since I broke with the Communists, ever since I left Poland. But do I have a choice? If it were simply myself, my own life, maybe I could convince myself that in the end it would be better to fold my arms, bow my head, and take what's coming to me. But I'm fighting for our people—our families, our friends, and those we don't know—because maybe they won't be granted either the time or the luxury of sitting back and waiting, doing nothing for victory, or peace, or universal redemption."

He poured himself a glass of water, then another. Drops of sweat were rolling down his forehead, his cheeks, right into his shirt collar.

"It's like this, my son: In Poland I believed in the revolution, and I could justify its violence. I told myself it was a necessary evil, an essential ingredient of victory. For a politically committed and motivated man it was a matter of principle, not sentiment. I repeated to myself the lessons the party had drummed into me: Since we have to use evil to destroy evil, it's better to do it with fervor and determination. And because the evil that confronts us is infinite, we must hunt it down beyond national frontiers, wherever we find it. And we must do this here and now."

That day Yoav's father had felt the need to confide in him. Why that day? Because he had just seen two Jewish boys killed by Palestinian saboteurs? Or just because Yoav, who had come home early from school, was standing there before him?

"Have I ever told you how I became a member of the party? It was because of my grandmother. She was a simple, taciturn woman. I believed she was invulnerable, stronger than an oak tree in the forest. She worked endless hours in rich people's homes to provide for her own needs (she would never accept help from her children) and those of friends poorer than herself. One evening when she came home she collapsed on her bed. The doctors diagnosed tuberculosis. At the time I didn't know what that meant. She died soon after, never having uttered a word of complaint. Some weeks later, a friend from the capital asked me if I knew what my grandmother had died of. 'Yes,' I told him, 'tuberculosis.' 'Do you know what that means?' 'No, not really,' I said. 'It means she died of hunger and humiliation.' "

Later, when Yoav himself became an officer, he vowed that he would accept hunger if need be, but never humiliation.

As for his father, when he reached old age, he came full circle, retracing his own parents' footsteps. He rediscovered the value, the beauty of their faith. He went so far as to visit the court of a Hasidic rebbe at Safed, who blessed him, praising his love for the Jewish people. "This love inside you," said the rebbe, laying his hands on the former Communist's shoulders, "will enable you to perform miracles. You will help our people overcome despair by celebrating joy and generosity, which have long been in exile, also awaiting their deliverance. And when this comes about, know that it is not you who have accomplished these miracles but the God of Abraham, Isaac, and Jacob. You are only his messenger."

So what if it is my turn? thought George Kirsten. I shall die sooner or later in any case. And what have I to lose? Pamela? She helps me to live, but she too will disappear one day. No, what matters is that the document should reach its destination. Everything else is unimportant.

With his wife, Marie-Anne, George had never known the happiness he had craved. There was no end to her recriminations, her glances, her countenance conveying regret and bitterness. "I should never have married you. We got married too soon," she would say. "Because of you, I've had no youth." Or else she would complain about his job, not adequately remunerated in her opinion. One pretext was as good as another, and Marie-Anne had many others. But the truth was simpler: They were not made for one another. There are people for whom happiness is poison; their natural element is mistrust; they prefer dreams to hopes fulfilled, mindful only of the cruelty of the gods rather than of their grace. Marie-Anne was like that. There had been too many misunderstandings between them, too many sleepless nights filled with remorse. Husband and wife could no longer lift a finger or utter a word without irritating one another. They no longer even tried to remember the harmony that had once nourished their love. Their bodies were no longer in tune. They resented each other's presence.

Fleeing the atmosphere of latent hostility and open resignation that reigned at home, their children lived their own lives far away. George recalled with bitterness that it was Paritus who had written, in a volume of meditations, "One of God's tragic jokes is to make you live with a woman who is not meant for you."

As an obscure public servant, George did not attract attention—monotonous work, modest salary. A social life with no surprises; a conjugal life with no pleasures.

He often asked himself how he could escape. But then his head would begin to ache until it almost blinded him. Had Pamela not been there with him at the office, and sometimes after work, he might well have taken his own life. The simplicity of this solution struck him forcefully one day: to end it all. Yes, to be done, once and for all, with this gray, dreary, depressing existence. Surely death gets rid of every problem; it puts an end to all adventures.

Yes, to end it all. Pamela would be unhappy but Marie-Anne, after a token tear of distress, would heave a sigh of relief: She would no longer feel watched, judged, indebted. She would no longer complain of living under constraint, in the shadow of real life. Would she be happier? Calmer? That, at least, would be something. Yes, if he died it would suit everybody, and him most of all. Farewell, everybody. He had lived long enough. Suffered enough. People would speak of him in the past tense: a few kind words, perhaps. Condolences. A fleeting effort to understand his weaknesses.

He was alone in his office. Outside, Washington was

beginning to come to life, vibrant, frantic, bubbling with political intrigues, both grand and sordid, with ludicrous and unwholesome plots designed to win an hour of influence, a fragment of power. Good God, whatever had possessed him to come to this city, where everyone is afraid of everyone, where life is made up of jealousy, ambition, and hypocrisy? He would have liked to find someone to run away with, to do something else, who knows, maybe scientific research. The sciences had interested him in his youth, astrophysics in particular. Ah, to be able to explore space, to speculate about the limits of the galaxies. . . .

Daily papers and journals piled up before him, waiting to be classified. Sometimes he filed them away without even reading them.

Outside, the sun was shining. The cherry blossoms were out. Tourists were strolling through the city's parks.

No doubt Marie-Anne had gone shopping. Nothing could stop her, neither rain nor snow. If she were the sole survivor of a nuclear holocaust, she would still go to the supermarket. And even if her husband gave her five servants, she would still make her solitary trips to the baker or the greengrocer. "Well, at least it keeps me in touch with my contemporaries," she often said, accusingly. As if George were not her contemporary. As if, deep in his archives and immersed in the past, he had lost all contact with the present.

If I die, thought George, will I bring her satisfaction at last? Will I be responsible for the happiness of at least one wife in this crazy world? What is dying? It is simply to conclude and say that the life you've lived has nothing to do with—with what? With happiness?

In one of Paritus's books, George had discovered a dialogue between the old mystic and a philosopher whose name he could not remember. It was a dialogue about death.

"To die is to give up waiting," Paritus says.

"But what about God? As he is above time, God waits for nothing. Does this mean that he too is dead?"

"You blaspheme, I pity you. I pity you because you are without hope. No, do not protest. I am not saying you are in despair; that is something else. To be in despair can be useful and fruitful; to live without hope is not."

"You have not answered my question: Since God lives outside time, how can he wait?"

"God is," replies Paritus. "God is both inside and outside time. That is to say, God lives in the passage of the one to the other. He is the incarnation of waiting. God is also the One whom we await."

In a document dating from the Russian Revolution, Pamela had shown George another dialogue about waiting. This one between two prisoners of the Okhrana, the czar's secret police.

"Yesterday when they brought you back, you were covered in blood. They'd been torturing you. How was it?"

"Hard, it was hard. Yet the torture itself is bearable; the worst is the anticipation."

"But then how did you survive? How do you manage to live like this, knowing you will be tortured again and again?"

"You cannot understand," came the reply. "A man who is fighting for the future of mankind is not waiting for torture, he's waiting for— the Revolution."

Strangely, these stories affect George now, although when he first read them they had left him indifferent.

A third story comes into his mind; he found it in a manuscript that was part of a valuable collection recently acquired by the National Library.

A winter night. In a noisy inn somewhere in the Carpathian mountains, an old rabbi, whose eyes are filled with gentleness, is chatting with a grinning Romanian officer. What can they possibly have to say to one another? They are discussing a prisoner. Iancu Stefan has got himself arrested, rather foolishly. Two drunkards had started a brawl. One of them pulled a kitchen knife; the other defended himself with his bare fists. The man with the knife got the upper hand. There he was, standing over his adversary—who was on his knees—ready to cut his throat. Incongruously dressed in peasant's clothes, Iancu Stefan intervenes to prevent the murder. Furious, the other drinkers insult him. Appearing from heaven knows where, a policeman sternly asks him what he is thinking of, disturbing the peaceful inhabitants of this hamlet. One word leads to another, and Iancu Stefan finds himself at the police station. In his pouch they discover false papers and compromising pamphlets. He is accused of being a Communist, a Jew, a spy, and a traitor. An officer from the city takes over the investigation: Who are his accomplices, his contacts? The interrogation involves threats, blows. But Iancu Stefan knows how to take punishment. His body is covered with bloody scars, but he doesn't utter a single cry.

Changing his tactics, the officer calls upon the village rabbi to use his spiritual authority and order the Jew to confess. The rabbi's reply is sophisticated. "Captain, either your prisoner is a Communist, in which case he will not recognize my authority, or else he is innocent, in which case you should let him go." The officer replies angrily, "He's a Communist, I tell you. Just take a look at the garbage he's been carting around."

The old rabbi obeys. He reads the tracts written in Yiddish, then reads them again. He appears confused. "There's no harm in this young man, Captain," he finally says. "These texts speak of fraternity and justice. Such noble ideals are to be found in our sacred books and indeed in yours." Then, understanding the ways of the Romanian administration, especially in the provinces, the rabbi uses a more convincing argument; he slips a few banknotes into the officer's hand. The latter is still not sufficiently convinced, so the rabbi adds a few more. "Right. Take him away and tell him not to do it again," mutters the officer in disgust.

The rabbi takes Iancu Stefan home with him, looks after him, and feeds him. One Sabbath evening the young Jewish revolutionary, whose real name is Shmuel Jacobovitch, says to him, "I'm not a believer. I observe neither the Sabbath nor the holy days. I don't follow the commandments. I'm hostile to religion. And yet you have helped me." The rabbi replies gently, "You are a Jew. Do I have the right not to come to the aid of my brother?"

"But I don't believe in God," cries Iancu Stefan.

"You don't believe, you don't believe. . . . But in spite of everything you are ready to suffer and perhaps to die for your own faith, your faith in History, as one of your pamphlets puts it, in the Revolution, in political action against our rulers. I believe in God and you believe in that which negates God. But if you had to choose between that officer with his power and myself, who have none, whom would you choose?"

Taken aback by the old rabbi's intelligence and generosity, Iancu stares at him intently before replying. "So, you think we might have something in common? And that we might both choose hope and its difficulties over cowardly submission to our oppressors?"

The rabbi smiles sadly. "For me, it's easy. The Torah continuously sustains me. It shows me my way, I am bound not to turn aside from it. But you, my brother, who shows you the way?" Iancu feels himself overcome with emotion. He suddenly feels very close to the old man. This surprises and disconcerts him. He ought not to feel close to a pious Jew who lives in the dark ages, who refuses to break the chains that shackle him and prohibit all progress to mankind. He ought to contradict him, ridicule him, urge on him the greatness of Marxist ideology and Leninist theory, and demonstrate to him their importance for all oppressed and humiliated peoples, including the Jews. But he is tongue-tied, and it is the old rabbi who breaks the silence. "You, my brother, are waiting for mankind to become better; I am waiting for the Lord to remember us. So why don't we wait together, what do you say?" Moved to tears, the liberated prisoner nods, as if he could hear the Jewish child within him replying *Amen*.

As for me, I'm waiting for nothing, George tells himself. He has never rebelled against anything or anybody. He had let Marie-Anne dominate him. He was born resigned. Even his affair with Pamela was more abdication than revolt. The discovery of the document and his journey to Israel? Until now he had believed this would be the great event of his life. But now it no longer seemed to have much importance. Whether the former Nazi had repented or not was not George's affair. The Nazi was not the only one to have made a travesty of justice, nor the worst. In any case, the Israeli researchers would do what was necessary.

Disillusioned, George had even lost his taste for discoveries. Life was going on without him, outside him.

He had not taken his life at other moments of despair: Suppose he did so now by offering himself as a volunteer? It would not be to save his traveling companions; he had no feeling for them whatsoever. So why would he do it? For whom?

For his children who lived so very, very far away?

George felt as if fists of steel were squeezing his throat. Bruce was hallucinating, seeing himself arraigned before a tribunal of dead women. Claudia was shivering, while Razziel addressed his last wishes to Kali. Alone at the window, Yoav remained lucid, tensed like a bow.

Into what nightmare had they plunged? Until now it was a psychodrama, soon it would become a nightmare.

Suddenly, a fierce and desperate cry made them start. It came from outside.

THE DIE is cast. No more doubts. No more memories prowling like criminals through their minds. The blank page, on which fate has scrawled its indecipherable writing, is turned. Soon the sacrificial slaughterer will appear; soon he will lead his victim to the altar. And the family of mankind will contain one assassin more and one human being less.

The night was coming to an end when the Hunchback opened the door. He was sneering, as if to hide—or emphasize—the suffering that marked his face. He looked as if he were about to laugh and cry at the same time.

The danger was taking shape. Now they were sure of it; they were about to witness an execution, a murder. The Judge had spoken of a game, but the Hunchback had not returned to play games.

So stressed was Razziel that when he looked at Claudia he did not recognize her; she strangely resembled Kali. Bruce made a tentative gesture, as if to keep the young woman away from him; she frightened him. Yoav, ready to hurl himself at the Judge when the door opened, let his arms drop when he saw the Hunchback: It's all over, he thought. George wrung his hands, shaking his head in disbelief. The tension increased several notches. A crazy thought flashed through Razziel's mind: And what if Paritus were there, close to him but in disguise? Claudia thought about David. She thought about him with such intensity that she felt her heart ready to burst.

She did not feel the Hunchback's stare. A fresh pain was rushing over him. He looked away hastily and began speaking, as if in a trance, standing on the threshold facing the five petrified hostages.

"The first time I saw her, it was the intensity of her yearning that struck me. And if I have finally found the strength within myself to resist and to rebel, it is on account of this woman, whose face and hair are the color of fire. I had noticed her yearning as soon as she came in. Who was it for? Not me. Me? I don't exist, not even in my own eyes. It was as though she were looking at someone behind me.

"I have never seen such yearning; it transformed her face and her body. She was no longer a woman like those that fill my dreams. She was not sad, not even melancholy; she was something else. She seemed to live elsewhere, deeply immersed in her own world, away from all pettiness. And, yes, I saw her, I saw this woman with my own eyes, I swear it.

"She had just arrived. I did not yet know who she was, I did not even know her name, but I knew everything about her, everything about her life, even the one she has not yet lived. I knew she both revealed and concealed herself in the reflection of her yearning. I knew I loved her. I understood it when I saw her lower lip tremble. What words was she murmuring? Was she uttering a plea? I loved her. That was all. That was enough. I never wanted to know anything else. There was nothing more to know.

"Why did she lean her head on her left shoulder? What was it about this shoulder that the other one, the right, didn't have? A crazy idea took hold of my imagination and projected it toward her. It was as if I myself were splitting in two. I saw myself getting up, leaving my place, and taking several steps toward her: I had to say something, something urgent, something true, something that could not wait. I had to say to her that nobody has the right to transform a stranger's life simply by daydreaming like that, with one's head resting on one's left shoulder. I had to tell her. . . . No, I would tell her nothing. Now I can see myself in front of her. I'm about to take her arm. I take it, I squeeze it very tightly, and I make her get up and follow me. It's a strange thing: No one pays any attention to us. We walk slowly, without a word; we walk toward the door, toward the life that awaits us on the other side, that awaits us within ourselves and . . . a terrible pain transfixed me. I was still sitting in my place, watching all of you; you talked and talked, and she talked too, but less than the rest of you. The dream had faded. Yet I still seek it and I shall find it. It is a part of me, it's in the reflection of that elusive and invasive *me* that you call consciousness. And there is consciousness in rejection."

The Hunchback broke off. He had spoken without pausing. His head bowed, he avoided the prisoners' eyes. Was he going to continue his monologue?

It was past six o'clock. Evidently indifferent to what the Hunchback was saying, Yoav had taken out his penknife to scrape away the hoarfrost that encrusted the windows. He could see nothing. Snow, two feet deep, covered the landscape. He was still wondering what mission the Judge had entrusted to the Hunchback. Who had been chosen to die? And how was the Hunchback going to go about it? Whatever his plan, Yoav had decided to stop him. If he invited him or one of the others to follow him outside, he would oppose it. Whatever happened, Yoav knew how to defend himself.

Bruce went over to Claudia but she ignored him. Like Yoav, she had her eyes fixed on the Hunchback.

And now the Hunchback began speaking again.

"The Judge was always a madman. Out of his mind. You must believe me. I have known him better than anybody. Didn't I tell you? I owe my life to him, but also my shame. He should have let me die, but he needed a humble and obedient slave. I was his thing. Thanks to me, he felt superior to God. He hid the sun from me and forbade me to dream; he was afraid I might escape.

"Year after year, he subjected me to torture he believed to be without precedent in the world. Sometimes he poured wine into me until I was crawling around on the ground like a pig. Or he would leave me out in the cold, half naked, so he could watch me shaking like a desiccated tree in the depths of winter. Or he would show me pictures of naked women to bring home to me what I would always be deprived of. Above all, he liked to talk to me about death—not about the death that awaited me but the one already within me. 'You're dead,' he kept telling me, 'but you don't know it.'

"Then, for a day or a week, I had to behave like a dead man among the dead, while he acted out the Resurrection and the departure from the tomb. He was Christ and I was one of the thieves crucified with him. Except that the Judge did not put the teachings of Jesus into practice, no way; he wanted to be a corrupted, malevolent Christ.

"One day I was a Roman soldier forcing the condemned men to climb onto their crosses before being torn apart by an angry crowd. Another day he said, 'I'm your father; you must get ready to kill me.' The next minute he accused me of being a parricide and beat me until I bled.

"Why did he commit all these cruel acts? He was mad, I tell you. Mad with black hatred, mad with unsated violence. Yesterday, during the storm, he was preparing for your arrival. He guessed that an airplane would land near here. He knew that its passengers would come and occupy this room. He was ready. And so was I.

"He told me about a command he had received in a dream, a divine command. You've heard it already. In order to save humanity from the ultimate punishment, heaven demanded a human sacrifice. 'You understand, my little hunchback,' he said, 'the only reason for this storm was to allow this sacrifice to take place. I shall take care of the trial and the verdict; you will execute the sentence.'

"This latest folly seemed to me more hideous—no, more real—than any before. He explained his plan to me in a calm, deliberate voice. Almost serene. He spoke in the name of bloodthirsty gods, he said, but he was not one of them. He was simply obeying orders. Their will must be done. Since they wanted the death of a human being, their representative's duty was to offer it to them. But—and he repeated this to me again, when he was briefing me just now—the scapegoat must not be burdened with sins. On the contrary, on this particular night, the chosen victim must be pure and innocent, no more deserving of death than anyone else. That is why my master was eager for you to make the choice yourselves. You were to become judges in your turn, judges of innocence, of the most innocent one among you.

"He said to me, 'Do you understand the honor that will fall to you? You will be the sacrificial priest, who brings the gods the offering they need in order to hold sway over the world of men. You will be their chosen one, their benefactor.'

"He sounded like a perfectly sane man, speaking in measured tones, but it was beyond my comprehension. What did he want, what did he expect of me? For me to kill someone? I, who hate death, having seen it from too close at hand? As in a trance, I fired rapid questions at him: How or with what did he want me to kill this someone? With a revolver? A rifle? Should I throw him or her into the flames of a burning building? Should I run over him or her in a car? Should I put him or her outside naked, to turn into a statue of ice?

"But at the same time I knew who it would have to be: the person who first caught my eye, the one among you who had filled me with yearning.

"And now the Judge handed me a huge knife. Heaven

knows where he unearthed it; at a butcher's shop in the village, no doubt. I've never seen one as big or as sharp in my whole life. He was holding it in his hands as if he were following some primitive ritual. 'Here's what you'll use to carry out the will of the gods,' he says to me. 'You'll go into the room, and you'll ask which of our guests has been chosen. If they refuse to reply, then you will choose: the first one to catch your eye. You will go up to this person and do what you have to do. Remember, you survived. And it was for this moment, in order to perform this act, that I saved you.'

"I have never heard him express himself with such icy sobriety. He had a clear vision of his purpose, I did not. Within me there was only disorder and chaos. Big words and little ones, gentle ones and terrible ones, swirled around in my brain, tearing it into a thousand pieces. The Judge, who was he really? Who was speaking through his mouth? And who was I? And where were we? Who was responsible for what was happening to us? And for the assassin I was about to become?

"Involuntarily, my head began moving, turning from right to left, from left to right, faster and faster. My head was saying *no,* and my heart too. My whole body was trembling and saying *no. No* to this madness, *no* to this idea, *no* to this order, coming from Death, which lurked beneath the mask of the Judge.

"But the Judge rejected my *no.* 'Don't be afraid,' he said. 'It's only a game, but a different game, a divine game, one commanded by the gods. It's their will you are opposing, don't you see? Who authorized you to disobey the gods who rule over men? Do you not fear their wrath, they who can overturn the laws of nature, and whose punishment can be terrible?'

"My head and my heart, my entire body, continued saying *no.* Until that moment I had always sought to please my master; I had submitted to every one of his whims, ever eager to give him yet another proof of my gratitude. But this, no. It's true I'm no angel; I've done stupid things, I've been an accomplice to his excesses, I've been a party to his follies. But now I had reached the limit. I would not cross the line.

"Suddenly I felt a violent need to do something I had never before had the courage to do. Whether in order to appease the gods or to defy them, whether to utter a shout of submission or one of blasphemy, I played with the idea that I might sacrifice myself there and then, become immortal, so that my blood would flow and the heavens might blush at the dawning of the day. But it was beyond my strength. I remained stock-still. I felt abandoned, useless, powerless.

"Meanwhile the Judge kept taunting me. Madness had seized him now. Like the air, the sea, or the breath of God, it became an all-enveloping tide that engulfed him. 'But it's so easy!' he exclaimed. 'It's so easy to take a man's life. Or a woman's, the most beautiful of women. Look, you take the knife. You lay it against the throat, so. You press gently, very gently, then harder, a bit harder. . . .'

"Was it I who unwittingly applied pressure?

"Was it he who unconsciously made one move too many?

"His cry, like that of a beast being slaughtered, brought me back to reality.

"Yes, the Judge's prediction was correct. He was right in telling you that a verdict would be brought in. What was it he said? That beneath this roof someone would die after day had dawned? Well, someone has died. Was it a game? For you, perhaps, but not for him.

"And not for me.

"The Judge has judged himself. And I was his executioner."

The teller of this tale is Razziel, who has woven into it the testimonies of his companions, who were all saved. After the Judge's death, the snowstorm abated. In the morning, taking advantage of the calm, cars hired by the airline plowed their way through the country roads, gathering up the dispersed passengers. No one was missing. The continuation of the flight took place without incident. The five survivors from the Judge's house exchanged addresses and promised to remain in contact. Claudia was reunited with David. George met "Boaz," who helped him hand over the document to the competent authorities. Yoav enjoyed another eighteen months of fragile happiness with Carmela. Bruce lost his cherished scarf. And the Hunchback? He went on living in the house of the Judge, whose death was recorded as "suicide."

As soon as the plane touched down at Lod Airport, Razziel took a taxi. He was in a hurry to get to Jerusalem. Even before leaving his things at the hotel, he made his way to the Old City with a thumping heart.

Naturally, old Paritus was not at the rendezvous. Razziel looked for him among the beggars who spend their days and nights beside the Wall. He questioned them, offering them money in exchange for information. He questioned the pupils of the Talmudic schools, the disciples of the visionary masters. None of them knew who he was talking about.

At the hotel, a letter from Paritus was waiting for him. He asked Razziel to excuse him, but he could not stay any longer. He had left the country on the eve of Razziel's arrival. The old mystic wrote:

> You are searching for your past, and you will continue to search for it. No one, not even God, can restore it to you. Sometimes it hides in the present, sometimes even in the future. But you should know that it, too, is searching for you, otherwise our meeting would never have taken place. Look around you: Every face you see offers an element that in some way attaches you to your past.
>
> Remember also that it is not knowledge but the yearning for knowledge that makes for a complete, accomplished man. Such a man does not stand still but perseveres in the face of adversity, nor does he remain untouched by the pain caused by absence. On the contrary, he recognizes himself in each cry, uttered or repressed, in the smallest rift, in the most pressing need.
>
> The rift within such a man, Razziel, is a grave one for, going beyond the limits of time, he too yearns for completeness. The prophet is a person who desires to be whole but is torn between God and man. The artist is whole, and yet, recognizing that time is at once his ally and his enemy, he can neither live nor create out-

side his own boundaries. The madman is whole, and yet it is the rift within his very being that renders him mad.

Searching for the past, and for its meaning, leads a man to discover distant worlds, perfectly organized, well structured, and often indecipherable, worlds where saints violate pregnant women; where children ridicule their parents; where you witness an occult transfusion of meaning from word to word, from brain to brain, all linked to a cosmic design imagined by God. But can one person's past take the place of another's? This is a question that will always fascinate the madman and the artist.

Like the madman, the artist substitutes one logic for another, invents characters, establishes new systems of values. The difference between them? The artist questions himself; the madman does not. The madman believes he is someone else. But each of them suffers from the same emotional distress; each feels cramped inside his own skin; each strives to escape his past in order to reinvent it in the prophet's agonizing silence.

And where does this leave you, Razziel?

Razziel rereads the letter several times. He is searching it for coded signals, the message within the message.

He thinks: Paritus is alive, that must suffice for now. Is he the reincarnation of the medieval writer mentioned by George Kirsten? God, give me some of his wisdom.

Later he will change that to: God, leave him his wisdom. Let him pursue his quest and I will continue mine. Will it help me to live my future, since I am incapable of living my past? Will it lead me to discover the shadowy events of my amputated life? Will I one day know what is hidden from me today?

The beginning will forever remain rooted in its own mystery.

A NOTE ABOUT THE AUTHOR

Elie Wiesel is the author of more than forty books, including his unforgettable international best-sellers *Night* and *A Beggar in Jerusalem,* winner of the Prix Médicis. He has been awarded the Presidential Medal of Freedom, the United States Congressional Gold Medal, and the French Legion of Honor with the rank of Grand Cross. In 1986, he received the Nobel Peace Prize. He is Andrew W. Mellon Professor in the Humanities and University Professor at Boston University. He lives with his wife, Marion, in New York City.

A NOTE ON THE TYPE

This book was set in Monotype Dante, a typeface designed by Giovanni Mardersteig (1892–1977). Conceived as a private type for the Officina Bodoni in Verona, Italy, Dante was originally cut only for hand composition by Charles Malin, the famous Parisian punch cutter, between 1946 and 1952. Its first use was in an edition of Boccaccio's *Trattatello in laude di Dante* that appeared in 1954. The Monotype Corporation's version of Dante followed in 1957. Although modeled on the Aldine type used for Pietro Cardinal Bembo's treatise *De Aetna* in 1495, Dante is a thoroughly modern interpretation of the venerable face.

Composed by Creative Graphics,
Allentown, Pennsylvania
Printed and bound by Berryville Graphics,
Berryville, Virginia
Designed by Virginia Tan